Lake Shore Return
A Redemption Shores Novel

JENNIFER RODEWALD

Rooted Publishing

Copyright © 2023 Jennifer Rodewald.

Print ISBN: 979-8-9874510-3-8

All rights reserved. No part of this publication may be reproduced, distributed, or transmitted in any form or by any means, including photocopying, recording, or other electronic or mechanical methods, without the prior written permission of the publisher, except in the case of brief quotations embodied in critical reviews and certain other noncommercial uses permitted by copyright law. For permission requests, write to the publisher, addressed "Attention: Permissions Coordinator," at the address below.

Any references to events, real people, or real places are used fictitiously. Names, characters, and places are products of the author's imagination, and any similarities to real events are purely accidental.

Front cover images from Shutterstock. Design by Jennifer Rodewald.

First printing edition 2023.

Rooted Publishing

McCook, NE 69001

Email: jen@authorjenrodewald.com

https://authorjenrodewald.com/

All Scripture quotations, unless otherwise indicated, are taken from the Holy Bible, New International Version®, NIV®. Copyright ©1973, 1978, 1984, 2011 by Biblica, Inc. Used by permission of Zondervan. All rights reserved worldwide. www.zondervan.com The "NIV" and "New International Version" are trademarks registered in the United States Patent and Trademark Office by Biblica, Inc.

CONTENTS

1. One — 1
2. Two — 4
3. Three — 15
4. Four — 25
5. Five — 30
6. Six — 39
7. Seven — 46
8. Eight — 56
9. Nine — 66
10. Ten — 72
11. Eleven — 84
12. Twelve — 94

13.	Thirteen	100
14.	Fourteen	107
15.	Fifteen	116
16.	Sixteen	122
17.	Seventeen	132
18.	Eighteen	143
19.	Nineteen	150
20.	Twenty	161
21.	Twenty-One	171
22.	Twenty-Two	181
23.	Twenty-Three	187
24.	Twenty-Four	194
25.	Twenty-Five	201
26.	Twenty-Six	206
27.	Twenty-Seven	213
28.	The End	220
29.	Teaser for Lake Shore Splendor	222

One

Hunter stumbled from his bed, aware of someone knocking at the door. Likely it was Lieutenant Commander Brighton, since it was Sunday evening. Was it still Sunday? How long had Hunter slept? Groping his dresser, he searched with eyes half-open for his phone. Once that was located, he checked the time—and the date. Yes. Sunday, 1830 hours.

Right on time as usual. Brighton always came on Sunday evenings, after his Bible thing—extra effort on his part, Hunter supposed, because the man attended at least one service at church on Sunday mornings with his family. That summed up Hunter's division commanding officer. Brighton was extra with everything. In a good way. Arrived on base early. Worked until every t was crossed and i was dotted. Walked in straight lines. Turned at ninety degrees. Always went above and beyond.

And he had taken an interest in Hunter.

Hunter wasn't sure why. He wasn't an outstanding lieutenant junior. He wasn't an outstanding anything. Generally, Hunter kept his head down and did what he was told. Stayed out of trouble and out of the spotlight.

But Lieutenant Commander John Brighton had taken notice of him anyway, and he had mysteriously invested in him. Not in a way that Hunter would have supposed a navy officer might do, however. Rather than calling him in to peptalk him on advancement or show him the possibilities of a naval-officer career, he showed up at Hunter's apartment on Sunday evenings, a box of wings in hand, a couple of beers, and a willingness to just hang out for a while. Before he left, he asked if he could pray for Hunter.

It was weird. But nice. And the prayers seemed sincere.

"Doesn't your wife mind you not being home on a Sunday evening?" Hunter had asked a couple weeks in to this strange but genuine offer of . . . friendship?

"She doesn't." His expression was honest while he answered. "Said to offer for you to come to Sunday dinner some afternoon after church, but you don't strike me as the overly social type, so how about we start with this?"

That had been a few months back. In that space of time, Hunter did go for a Sunday dinner and met the easygoing Victoria Brighton, who had entertained him with stories of their two now-college-age kids, complete with pictures and keepsakes. It'd been a nice time, and enlightening. Hunter hadn't much experience with the classic American family—a mom, a dad, and a pair of kids, all living in apparent harmony. He'd grown up with mostly grief, isolation, and disfunction. Witnessing the Brighton family had been . . . interesting.

If he was honest, it had been soul stirring. It made Hunter wonder if *his* life could ever be that way. Harmonious. Joyful.

Complete.

A fresh set of pounding at the front door—this time louder—summoned Hunter back into the present moment. The one in which he felt like he'd been hit by a train and all he really wanted was to crawl back under his covers and lose consciousness until the aching went away.

Shaking his head, he found he'd shut his eyes as he'd braced himself against the dresser. His head pounded something fierce, every muscle in his body hurt, and breathing was painful. He shivered in the dimness of his bedroom.

That morning, when he'd tried to start his day, he had made it to the bathroom and then straight back to bed. Hadn't even opened the blinds to let in the spring sunshine. Somehow that morning sun had nearly made its full trek across the sky, and Hunter hadn't even made it out of the gym shorts he'd slept in yet. Had it been a chilly day?

Another shiver rippled through his body. Man, he was *so* cold.

Hunter fisted his phone and hugged his shoulders as he stumbled back to his bed. He'd text Brighton, let him know he wasn't feeling well. Just . . . right after he warmed up a minute.

Burrowing deep into his covers, Hunter's whole body quaked as he pressed into the mattress. He shut his eyes, willing away the deep pain behind his forehead. Drawing a long breath, he noticed again a sharp stab in his lungs.

But he'd be okay. In just a minute. He'd send Brighton a text, sleep off this bug, and start a new week tomorrow.

His muscles stopped trembling, and Hunter exhaled a wheezing breath, and then, blessedly, the shadow of sleep overtook him.

Two

Hazel scuffled off the ridge and onto the trail, Scout jogging down the steep rock path behind her. The air still held a hint of frost as she breathed out puffs of white, but the snow on the ground was more slush than fluff.

Spring had finally come. Up here on the mountain, it would be a gloriously long affair of below-freezing nights, progressively earlier sunrises, and days that would gradually reach above fifty degrees, a process that would follow the calendar well into June.

The thick sheet of ice on the lake would continue to crack and groan. The sound was unsettling to some—Bennett startled every time a sharp pop split through the canyon—but to Hazel it was the music of the changing season. The land would slowly awaken. Aspens would go from cracking buds of bright chartreuse to opening their fresh, leathery deep-green leaves to gather sustenance from the strengthening warmth of the longer, sunnier days. The marsh grasses along the shoreline would green up and begin their summer growth, inviting her horses, as well as the deer, elk, and moose, to fatten up after a long, cold winter.

Changing seasons.

While Hazel had always enjoyed the dependable cycles of nature, this year it was emotional. Because of Bennett. Her life had changed so much because of him. Usually, that was astonishing—in a good way.

Occasionally, it was unnerving. Hazel had never done well with change.

Reaching the bottom of the ridge, she paused to take in the view. Orange and yellow bounced off the waters, reflecting the late-evening colors of the sky. This would forever be her favorite time of day—and she'd been able to share it several times with Bennett over the past few months. He had made the trip to see her at least twice a month since January, and she'd visited him in the dizzying chaos that was Chicago several times in that span.

Janie said that must be love.

Hazel couldn't deny it. But there was an element of discomfort there.

She hadn't imagined love like this, and Hazel wasn't sure what to think or feel about that. This was a life she'd never envisioned—shared more and more with a man who unsettled her peace as much as he anchored her heart.

As she stood in the glory of the sunset, her heart and mind traveled back to the night Bennett had told her he was moving. Held securely against him, she had been enjoying the now-familiar scent of cloves and vanilla—*the smell of Bennett*, as she'd come to think of it. He'd kissed her temple and shifted her in his embrace so that he could nudge her face up to look at him.

Oh, how she could get lost in those dark-blue eyes. Especially when they held that sort of gaze on her.

"I love you, Hazel," he'd whispered, emotion carving deep into his whisper.

She had shut her eyes and savored that thrill. *Loved.* Something she'd never hoped for.

Bennett had moved again, propping his arm against the mattress beneath them and then leaning his head against his hand. With his free fingers, he traced the outline of her face. When next he spoke, his voice lost the whispered wonder and instead became something firmer and more convicted. "This isn't good enough for me though."

Her eyes flew open, and she searched his expression while her heart pounded wildly. "What do you mean?"

He shook his head, and a sad sort of pain caused his brow to furrow. Deep down she knew why. In the beginning he had paid for a hotel room for her visits, and he had intended to keep things that way. She had been the one to push for this physical intimacy.

It bothered him.

She had known it from that first shared night. The way he had been quiet and withdrawn after. He had acted like . . . Well, she wasn't sure like what. It had provoked a quarrel the next morning.

"It's like I'm a disappointment, Ben. That's devastating."

Those beautiful blue eyes sheened, and he shook his head as he dropped onto his leather couch. "That's not anywhere close to the truth. I am disappointed in me, not you. I want to be a better man, and this isn't how I wanted things to go between us."

"You think we've done something wrong?"

"I think that I've taken something that doesn't belong to me."

She sat back, offense coursing through her. "Belong to you? What does that mean? You think I should belong to you? Like a possession?"

"No." He jammed forked fingers into his hair, frustration in his look. "Like the greatest treasure a man could find."

"What is that?"

"A wife. A partner in life." Bennett's gaze held steady for a heartbeat, and then he folded his hands, leaned elbows against knees, and looked toward the floor beneath his bare feet. *"I wanted to wait . . ."*

Hazel had stared at him, befuddled. This was . . . historical? Patriarchal? She didn't know what—but she felt pretty certain most people didn't think that way. Probably. Then again, she didn't deal with people much, so what did she really know?

She knew she didn't want to feel like a possession. She didn't want to be held in anyone's grip. Not even Bennett's.

"I know I'm not your first, Bennett." Her words shot from her tongue like a poison dart. She felt immediately sorry for it.

Pain filtered into the heated glance he shot toward her. Then he nodded again, his shoulders rounding further. "You're right. I already told you that I'm not proud of the man you first knew me to be. But I wanted to do better. To be better." When he turned to catch her eye again, there was torture in his expression. *"For you. For us."* His hand swallowed hers and held tight. *"I want this to last."*

Hazel hadn't known how to argue with that. Especially when she had intentionally poked at something she had known would hurt him. She wanted what they had to last too. But she didn't see why sharing a bed would put that in jeopardy.

Ultimately, the discussion had died. And Bennett had given up on the hotel room for her when she visited.

That brought them to the night he'd said what they had wasn't good enough for him. Panic had threatened to take her captive—a feeling that was way too similar to the one of being trapped. Hazel hated it.

She reached to finger the hair just above his ear. "I love you too, Bennett. Please don't—"

He took her hand and brought it to his lips, kissing her fingertips. "I'm not. But I want more."

More? As in marriage? *I feel like I've taken something that doesn't belong to me . . .* His tortured explanation came as plain as if he'd just spoken them fresh. He wanted a wife, a partner in life. His words.

She'd never wanted to be a wife.

In Bennett's embrace, part of her thrilled at the thought. Most of her, however, cowered. On the whole, she had little exposure to such an arrangement. The one marriage she'd had an up-close view of—her grandparents'—didn't leave her with a desire to try it for herself.

Bennett wouldn't understand that, though that seemed bizarre to her. He'd seen his own parents' marriage go up in flames, so it seemed like he might get her point of view. By this reemerging conversation, he didn't.

"I've been looking into Bozeman." Bennett spoke into her whirling thoughts, startling her out of the fearful storm the thought of marriage had stirred up.

"Bozeman? Montana?"

He nodded. "The housing market is expanding. I could invest there."

"Oh." Her sigh was part relief and part confusion. Did this have anything to do with their relationship not being enough for him? Or had he changed the subject?

"Staci is competent. She can manage the Chicago office. I . . . I could move. To Montana."

Ah. Not a change of subject. A compromise?

She lifted her chin, her gaze traveling up from his chest to the eyes she loved so well. "You would do that?"

"To be close to you?" He leaned in but waited for her nod. Then his lips brushed against her brow. "I would do anything, Hazel. If it meant that you would trust my love."

"I do trust your love."

He pulled back, taking her hand again. Silently, he touched the emptiness of her left ring finger. And left the rest unsaid.

That had been two weeks ago. Within days he had signed a lease on a house in Bozeman, put his condo up for sale, and was currently in the process of investing in a property to flip. It was all fast and furious. And overwhelming.

A bird flitted across the darkening sky, calling out a bold song as it landed in a pine across the rippling water. Hazel came back into the present. Into the enjoyment of this sunset and the quiet peace and security that was her lake. The steadiness of a life that felt solid and unmoving beneath her boots.

Here, life made sense. Here, it was a thing she could manage. She felt in control.

She was happy that Bennett was selling his Chicago condo—heaven knew she never wanted to go back to the city again if she could help it. Bennett of Bozeman sounded much better than Bennett of Chicago to Hazel of Elk Canyon. He'd be within a two-hour drive—and he had already purchased the vehicle to make that trek. Not to mention, had talked her into having the north ridge road plowed and cleared so that he could drive that new Ford Bronco all the way to the lake, rather than trekking through the snow with a dog sled, as she had done her whole life.

Changes. But those were manageable changes.

Bennett made her happy. His smile warmed her clear through, and those dark-blue eyes made her tummy clench in the most addictive way—and who knew that was even possible? He could make her laugh. He treated her with respect and tenderness—another something Hazel hadn't known could be so. And when he held her, kissed her . . . All she knew was that she never wanted that feeling to go away.

Hazel blew out a long, slow breath, creating a small trail of white against the graying air.

Tired of sitting, waiting patiently for her master to give her the *go* sign, Scout popped off her backside and wagged her tail.

Hazel looked down at the mutt and grinned. "Time to go find your brothers?"

The dog gave her a happy yip.

Hazel waved her hand forward. "Go on then. Let 'em know I'm coming."

Her ears stood up straight, twitched, and then Scout yipped again. Then she was off, running the dirt path that wound from the west side of the lake, around the south, and led to the cabin. It was a half mile at least, but Scout would no doubt sprint the whole way. Hazel was not about to do that. She moseyed with a much less hurried pace. After ten minutes she rounded the southern bend, and her cabin came into view. A low, purposeful bark reached her as she passed the dock. Moose, her massive old friend.

"I'm coming, Moose," Hazel answered. As she did, the phone in the deep inner pocket of her warm winter coat dinged repeatedly.

Someone was blowing up her text app. Her first guess would have been Bennett, but he wasn't likely to send text after text like that. He would usually send one, then wait for her to respond, because he knew she was often outside of service.

Also, maybe it wasn't a series of texts. Those usually vibrated, come to think of it.

Curious, Hazel fished the phone from the pocket as she reached the steps to the front porch. Mindlessly, she patted Moose and tapped to unlock her phone.

No, those hadn't been a string of texts. They had been missed calls. A dozen of them over the past two hours. All from the same number—but not one she recognized.

Scowling at the oddity, Hazel tapped the voicemail icon and saw that she only had two messages there. Leaning against the deck rail, she pressed Play and the Speaker icon and listened to the unfamiliar voice.

"Miss Wallace, this is Dr. Sharpton at Banner Churchill Community Hospital. I need to speak with you as soon as possible. Please call me."

Banner Churchill Community Hospital? Where was that, exactly? Why would a doctor need to speak with her?

She moved to the next message and tapped Play. "Miss Wallace, this is Dr. Sharpton again. I am the attending physician for your brother, Hunter, and you are his only listed next of kin. Please call me."

As she listened to that message play out, her heart rate spiked. Attending physician for Hunter? Why did Hunter need an attending physician? Why did he need any sort of physician at all?

Panic rolled through her veins, hot and throbbing. She switched back to the call screen, hit the missed number, and tapped Send. The phone on the other side rang four times before somebody named Anita answered.

"I need to talk to Dr. Sharpton."

"I'm sorry. Dr. Sharpton is not on the floor right now."

"He'd better get on real quick. He left me a couple of messages, and I missed at least a dozen calls from him. Said it was about my brother, Hunter Wallace. I need to talk to him."

"Oh. Hang on one second." Anita put Hazel on hold.

The music reaching her ears was horribly irritating and did nothing to ease the racing pulse in her veins. Suddenly this promise of the soon-to-be-spring day turned less glorious. The hope of the coming days turned into something that felt cold and constricting. She hated that feeling. It was too much like the awful sensation of being trapped.

The last thing Hazel ever wanted to feel again was trapped.

Hazel stalked her way to her front door, which she nearly ripped open before she stormed into her cabin. This was taking way too long to talk to the doctor. What the heck was going on? Wasn't the military supposed to contact her if Hunter had been in an accident? How had he gone from doing whatever it was he did on base to needing an attending physician in a hospital, and she had known nothing about anything that had happened to get him there?

"Ms. Wallace?"

Finally. "That's me." Hazel gripped the back of the nearly ancient sofa in her living room.

"This is Dr. Sharpton."

"Good. What is going on with Hunter?" She saw no reason to practice what her nana would have called "polite conversation." She'd never been good at such a thing in the first place, and this was a get-to-the-point situation.

Dr. Sharpton cleared his throat. "Hunter was brought in this morning by ambulance. He's been sick—I'm not sure how long. His commanding officer said he'd been AWOL for two days before he finally broke into his place to check on him."

"Sick?"

"Yes. Quite sick with a respiratory illness. It hit hard, by the looks of it. His O2 sats were dangerously low when he arrived. His x-rays show spots in his lungs. We have him on oxygen, and I am monitoring his kidney and liver functions closely. I believe he is stable right now, but we wanted you to know."

"We?"

"Lieutenant Commander John Brighton—the officer who broke into his place to check on him this morning—and myself. It seems that you are all Hunter has."

Hazel stepped around the sofa and then sank onto the cushions. Those words . . . they were hauntingly familiar. Bennett had said them to her—or something similar to them—when he had been urging her to reach out to Hunter. Hazel had stubbornly refused. No amount of pleading, mild scolding, or—eventually when they were face to face—scowling from Bennett had changed her mind.

She'd even refused to see Hunter when he flew into Bozeman for twenty-four hours to help Bennett move into his new place. Outright, dug-in-her-heels-and-would-not-budge refused.

He's the only brother you have, Zel. And your only family.

Bennett had been disappointed in her, and he didn't try to hide it. She'd been mad at him for it—for interfering, and for taking Hunter's side, and for making her feel bad.

Yeah, she and Bennett had some issues. Hazel had limited experience with any type of relationship in general, so she wasn't sure what to do with that. Or even to know if it was normal or not. So mostly she left them alone and hoped they'd disappear on their own. Because no matter how frustrated he made her and she made him, she knew she was better with him than without. He connected her to a life she hadn't known she was missing, and she didn't want to lose that.

She didn't want to lose Bennett.

And Hunter? She'd never considered the possibility of losing him. Not for forever. Now she felt wretched about refusing to see or even speak to Hunter. Bennett had been right—Hunter was her only living family, and as of that moment, he lay in a hospital and some stranger had to call and tell her he was sick. Worse, the last conversation she'd had with her brother had been on the dark side of ugly, because she'd been livid. Not only had he sent a weasely version of Bennett Crofton to scope out her land with the intent to buy it out from under her boots, but Hunter had seen to it that she had gone to jail when he found out the sort of stunt she'd pulled on a memory-wiped and helpless Bennett.

Hunter hadn't been sorry for either of those offenses, and she saw no reason to forgive him. Hadn't mattered how much her pretend-husband-turned-angry-victim-turned-kind-boyfriend Bennett Crofton had pleaded with her to find a way to reconcile. Hazel wasn't having it. She wasn't the forgiving type, and she didn't see a problem with that.

Hunter had offenses to pay for, and she was going to make dang sure he did.

Except, she hadn't predicted this. Hunter in a hospital? Possibly close to death? Suddenly her vison cleared with jarring sharpness. Now her brother was hundreds of miles away, and they had never made their peace.

How was she going to live with that for the rest of her life?

"Ms. Wallace? Are you still with me?"

"Where is Banner Churchill Community Hospital?"

"Fallon, Nevada."

Nevada? Hunter was on a naval base in a landlocked state? There was such a thing?

"Did you not know where your brother was stationed?"

No, she hadn't known where Hunter was for the past six months or better. Hadn't bothered to ask. Last she had known, he was doing something on carrier ships, which she had assumed floated on a big blue ocean and ported in a state that held within its borders some sort of bay.

Hazel knew next to nothing about the navy, and she'd never cared to learn. Most especially when Hunter had announced that he'd applied and been accepted into their NROTC program and that was how he was getting through college.

She'd hated everything about that situation. Still did.

"I . . ." Did she owe this doctor an explanation? Surely not. The battle between her and her brother was not this stranger's business.

Once again the man on the other end of the line cleared his throat. "We wanted to make sure his family knew."

"We . . . you and the officer?"

"Correct. John Brighton. He'll likely reach out to you—I assume he hasn't yet already."

"No." Not that she knew of. Maybe she needed to scan those numbers more closely. Were they *all* the same?

"Miss Wallace, I'm not going to pry, as family is complicated, but life is unpredictable. And when it's gone, that's it. There's not a reset button."

Hazel drew back, as if the man had reached through the digital air and smacked her. "What does that mean?"

"It means that I've been in medicine a long time. I've seen it before—family members, for whatever reason, letting their kin die alone. I can tell you this—they almost always regret it."

Hazel's stomach dropped hard. *Die alone*? "Is Hunter going to die?"

"I can't make promises, miss." He paused, then added into the lengthening silence, "Either way don't let the past lead to further regrets."

Three

Bennett wiped the sweat from his face with a towel, then reached to shake the offered hand of his opponent. He hadn't played much racquetball since college, but given he was in a new town, with a mostly new life and no friends, he had joined a club and then signed up for their league.

It had helped. Some. Starting over was just hard. He'd known that going into it.

The shift of his life's plans rubbed a little raw against his comfort—not that he regretted this choice. In the weeks since he'd moved, he was finding his way into something that resembled a normal routine. Something that felt like firm footing—and if he was honest, it had been a long time since he'd felt that. Much longer than since he'd met the woman who had turned his world upside down. So he had solid ground beneath him and a developing life map. Both good things.

And racquetball was fun, especially when paired against José. The man was easygoing and funny, a good athlete but not overly competitive.

"Have plans for lunch?" José slid their handshake into a fist bump.

"Not anything that can't be changed." Bennett picked up the racket he'd set on the bench. "Did you have something in mind?"

"Yeah. That sandwich place a few blocks over is pretty good, if you're up for it?"

"Sounds perfect." Bennett slipped his four-week-old racket into its protective carrier, zipped the side, and flung the sweat towel around his neck. "Mind if I grab a quick shower first? I've got a property to look into at three."

"No problem." José motioned toward the locker room, and the pair wandered down the hall together.

Within twenty minutes, Bennett met José at the front doors of the athletic club, and they walked toward the parking lot.

José pointed out his vehicle—a 1990s Ford truck that had a vinyl sticker on the back window, of a cross and a cowboy. "That's me. Just follow my path down main, and I'll meet you."

"Will do." Bennett unlocked his Bronco with his key fob.

The sandwich place was all small town. Made Bennett think of the general store at Luna—small, simple, but enough. It also made him miss the people he'd come to think of as friends in that tiny town that. Mama Bulldog—who was as tough as granite, as smart as anyone he'd ever met, and loved big. Her daughter Janie—who made outstanding apple pie and was *usually* all bright sunshine and cheer. Jeremy Yates, the town sheriff and old friend of Hunter and Hazel's and seemed genuinely concerned for both.

And Hazel. Especially Hazel. He always missed her when she wasn't with him. Which seemed like a funny twist of fate since his fully restored memory could now recall how he felt about her when they'd first met.

The badger lady. That was what he'd labeled her.

Back then she had been less than impressed with him as well. A lot could change in a week . . . even more in several months.

In that span of time he'd discovered the prickly woman he'd initially disliked was actually a warm, tender heart hiding beneath a tough-as-nails exterior. She was in many ways his opposite—introverted and outdoorsy. But they shared more than they didn't. They both liked evenings together snuggled by a warm fire. Reading—specifically Sherlock Holmes. Scrabble. Natural beauty. Finding ways to make things work.

And they both wrestled with the complications of strained family relationships.

More than all that, though, they shared a growing attachment to each other, evidenced by multiple daily phone calls, ongoing texts threads, and several trips—every one of them a general inconvenience he and Hazel would have both avoided under *normal* circumstances—just to be together. Proof enough they were in this for the long haul.

He was definitely in this for the long haul.

Even though his new location was significantly closer to the woman who had wrangled his heart in the most unpredictable way ever, Bennett missed Hazel with increasing intensity. He wanted so much more than what they had right now, which was still basically a long-distance relationship.

If only she was up for it too. She confused him. Confounded him. But he'd known from the start she was an unusual and complicated woman. One who bewitched him and had taken his heart captive.

"Cowboy panini, side of fried pickles?"

The call from the counter drew Bennett out of his head and from the longing that made anxiety stretch tight in his chest. "That's me."

The girl with dark hair and hungry eyes tilted her face at him, her mouth tipped with a subtle Mona Lisa smile. Bennett knew that look—the one of feminine appreciation. And interest. Definite interest. In another life—one not so very long in his past—he would have capitalized on such a flirty look. By the end of lunch, he'd have known the pretty, barely-twenty-something's name and phone number, and he'd have taken that appreciation as far as she would have allowed.

A lot of times, that was way further than it ever should have gone.

A painful twist shot through his gut. Man, how had he gotten that selfish, that lost? Another stab sank into his stomach, and Bennett knew exactly why. He'd come a long way since his head injury had jarred him into conviction. But there were still things in his life that he needed to work on . . .

"Trout basket with a side of slaw?" That same pretty girl called out José's order.

The man stepped forward to grab it. If he appreciated the young woman's looks, he didn't show it. Might have something to do with the ring on his left hand.

Taking his food toward an empty table, Bennett exhaled a sigh. The apostle Paul's words from Romans drifted through his mind. *I do not understand what I do. For what I want to do I do not do, but what I hate I do.*

Lowering to the bench of the booth, Bennett shot a quick prayer up to heaven. *Help me be the man I should be . . .*

It would help if he and Hazel were on the same page. *That, Lord. Can you fix that part?*

José slid onto the bench across from Bennett, removed his ball cap, and inhaled the wafting aroma of his food. "Awww yeah." He grinned. "Mind if I send a quick thank-you to my heavenly Pappy?"

Bennett's suspicions were confirmed—José was a man of faith. Gratitude eased the tightness remaining in his chest. He sure could use a friend who shared his reemerging beliefs. One who could possibly help him find his way back fully into who he had wanted to be.

Bennett nodded. "I'll join you in that."

José thanked God for the food and good play. Bennett silently thanked Him for the provision of José.

"What brought you here?" José took a bite of a slender fried trout and leaned his elbows against the table.

Though the question was mere curiosity and nothing probing, Bennett stared at José, feeling caught in the keen discomfort of manly vulnerability. Was he gonna play this off as a new adventure? Something he'd wanted to try for a while—an escape from the big city to see how rural life set with him?

He'd been working hard to become the honest man he'd wanted to be back before he became a slimy image of the man who had been the greatest disappointment in his life. Lying now wouldn't help him be a better guy.

So just admit the truth? Man, that felt so awkward.

He couldn't say why, and the words wouldn't leave his mouth as he stared across the table, his posture rigid and throat tight.

A knowing look entered José's expression, amusement flickering in his dark eyes. One corner of his mouth slid upward, and he chuckled. "A woman, eh?"

Bennett exhaled, that feeling of being caught settling with less discomfort than moments before. Hadn't he just thanked God for a new friend? Perhaps he should put a little more faith in that gift.

"Yeah. I turned my life upside down for a woman. Moved from Chicago, entrusted the lucrative business I built from the ground up to my assistant, and am basically starting over in the wilds of Bozeman, Montana. All because of a little mountain lioness named Hazel Wallace." He selected a fried pickle from the food basket and popped it into his mouth. "A little nuts, right?"

José shrugged, good-natured laughter lighting his expression. "She must be something. Is it love?"

"She's not like anyone you've ever met before. I don't mean just any woman you've ever met, but any person. Ever. She's wild and independent and asocial and could drive you nuts within an hour." Bennett felt the intensity of his emotions in his voice. That list he'd just laid out were the things he loved about Hazel. And the same things that made him crazy. He sat back and shrugged, hoping to shed the tension that had just built.

"But yeah. I love her. I'm going to marry her. Someday." Bennett's confidence waned as he finished that last part. "I hope."

"You hope? Someday?" José shook his head. "Aye. That's a little vague for a guy who just moved halfway across the country."

Shoulders rolling in, Bennett looked toward his food and nodded. "Yeah. Things are . . . complicated. Hazel is complicated." He raised his eyes to find José's still steady on him. Listening with empathy. That was encouragement enough for Bennett to continue. "Trust is hard with her. And she's content with things between us the way they are now. So . . . I guess that's where we are. For now." He shrugged.

José's slow nod was understanding yet guarded. "This world seems to offer all sorts of opportunities for scars, doesn't it?"

"That's a good way of putting it."

Leaning back, José folded muscled forearms across his chest. "I will pray for you, then, mi amigo."

Tension unfurled from Bennett's shoulders. "I would appreciate that." Once again he dared to look the other man in the eye. Yes, for certain they shared a brotherhood. The Spirit within Bennett confirmed it. *Sons of God in Christ.* A first for Bennett—this strong connection. The last bit of hesitation to be real with José melted. "More than you know, I need it."

José nodded, and somehow Bennett knew it was as good as done. One more confirmation that this life change was for Bennett's good. *And Hazel's. Please, God. Reach her heart with Your goodness too.*

Bennett blinked into the bright sunshine as he stepped out of the heavy double doors of the church. Turning, he craned his neck to gawk at the stonework that made up the cross tower at the front of the building. Pale sandstone rose in a patchwork of backbreaking work and craftmanship, rising above the dark-gray peak of the main building's roof.

He liked architecture. And beauty. This building had both. And with the blue-and-gray backdrop of the majestic mountains, the setting had a breathtaking quality.

More and more Bennett liked this move to Bozeman. Slower paced, less frantic living, significantly less population and congestion. And the main draw—Hazel was an easy two-hour drive away.

Then there was this unexpected bonus.

He dropped his appreciative gaze from the apex of the cross tower and turned to smile at José, who had exited the building right behind him. The man's easy invitation to church was yet another promising sign of a better future to come.

"It was a good service, right?" With a Bible tucked in one hand, José held out his free hand, and Bennett clasped it.

"It was." Bennett felt the absence of his own copy of God's Word. Man, he was still so out of practice with the going-to-church thing. Back in Chicago the church he'd attended after the new year typically only looked at one or two verses per service, and they always threw those words up on the big screen. He hadn't felt a whole lot of need to bring his own copy.

Here? They had read a full Psalm at the beginning of service, every attendee standing in honor of God's Word as they held open their own copy to read from. Then there was the music—during which two more selected passages were read. And then the sermon, which was a continuing study in Philippians. The pastor had invited the congregation to open their Bibles and read along as he read the full chapter from which his study would come—and he waited while the people turned there.

Long story short, Bennett had wished he'd brought his Bible. And next week he would.

"There's a whole lot of anxiety in our lives, isn't there?" José carried the conversation forward. "Man, I'm bad at trusting God's plans for good."

Savoring the late-morning sun on his back, Bennett shoved his hands into his khaki pockets and nodded. "Same. I'll be thinking about that this week."

That wasn't hyperbole. Ever since the accident that had cleared his memory for a time and then reminded him of who he'd once hoped to be, Bennett had struggled with worry. What if it was too late for him? What if he'd already screwed up his life too much?

What if he was still screwing it up because he lacked the resolve to be better?

That one. That one kept him up long into the night many times, as he longed for Hazel in his arms and then felt profound guilt that he'd already taken what wasn't rightfully his—and wasn't being a godly example to her beautiful, lost heart.

I'm still screwing it all up—and taking her down with me!

And yet he continued. What was wrong with him?

"I'm glad you came," José said, drawing Bennett away from the spiraling thoughts that plagued his peace. "And that I can introduce you to my wife." With a grin that read proud peacock, and a side look at the short dark-haired woman at his side that proclaimed completely-in-love-and-not-ashamed-of-it, José slid his hand around that woman's and lifted it up to kiss her knuckles. "This is Rosalina." He gazed down at her as if she was his world. "Isn't she the loveliest woman you've ever seen?"

Bennett cleared his throat.

Rosalina smiled softly but pushed against her husband's chest. "How is he supposed to answer that, José?"

José merely chuckled.

Sliding her hand free, she held it out to Bennett. "You don't need to. But it is very nice to meet you, Bennett Crofton. José had mentioned you several times."

With a cocked brow tipped toward José, Bennett shook Rosalina's hand. "Has he?"

"A God calling. That's what he tagged you with."

"Not sure how I feel about that."

"If God has called another to invest in you, I think you should feel honored," Rosalina said. "After all, isn't it amazing that the Creator of all things not only *sees* you but wants you to know it?"

Though a touch of heat brushed his face, Bennett chuckled. "Good point."

"Beautiful and smart. I hit the jackpot, right?" José said.

"Oh, José, stop it."

A younger woman strode to José's side and stopped to look up at him with a mocked scowl. "You're such a sap. What would Pappy say?"

"He would only argue that Mama is the prettiest and the smartest." With his Bible still in hand, he tucked this new girl under his arm and squeezed. "Bennett, this is my baby sister, Isabelle. Isa, meet Bennett Crofton."

Large dark eyes, framed by impossibly long black lashes, looked up at him, and appreciation for what she saw gleamed without censor. "Hello, Bennett."

With an uneasy glance at José, Bennett reached to shake his sister's hand. "It's nice to meet you, Isabelle."

"Isa," she repeated, grinning.

"Easy, Isa." José shook her gently. "He moved to Bozeman from Chicago to be closer to his girlfriend."

The younger woman's eyes gleamed with good-humored mischief. "Lucky girl." She winked and then scooted away. "See you back at the ranch," she called over her shoulder.

Bennett muffled a relieved sigh.

"She's twenty-two and boy crazy," Rosalina said.

"Eyah-eye." José rolled his eyes.

Rosalina patted her husband's arm. "But a good girl."

"So far."

Letting that slide unanswered, Rosalina turned to Bennett. "Will you be joining us for lunch?"

"Uh . . ." He hadn't known that was an option.

"You don't want to miss lunch at the Romeros'." José tipped his head sideways and turned to walk toward the parking lot.

Bennett had no doubt that was true. It would be better than drive-thru and spending the afternoon alone scrolling through properties for sale. "I'll take you up on that."

He followed the happy couple as they made their way to a red Ford SUV—a significantly newer and nicer vehicle than what José drove around town in. Conveniently, Bennett found he'd parked only three cars away.

The phone in his back pocket buzzed just as Bennett was going to lift his hand and say *lead the way*. He checked it, thinking he'd let voicemail take the call.

But it was Hazel.

Holding up one finger, Bennett called to José, "Give me a minute, will you?"

José nodded.

Bennett turned to answer the phone. "Hi, pretty mountain lion."

"Hi, city boy."

Something in her voice put him on high alert. Bennett leaned against his car, knowing he wasn't going to the Romeros' that afternoon.

Four

Hazel didn't give in to impulses. Not usually. The last time she had, she'd ended up with a not-real husband who couldn't remember his own name. And that little impetuous stunt had landed her in jail.

Impulses didn't end well.

With that in mind, she had sucked in a deep breath, poured a strong brew of mint tea, and sat on the braided rug in front of the empty fireplace to talk things out with Moose.

"He's sick, old man. Your boy is sick and in the hospital. What should I do?" She swallowed against the swell in her throat. Burying her hand into the thick, long masses of the Great Pyrenees's fur, she leaned down and pressed her head against his neck. "I'm still so mad at him! He left us. Betrayed us." A quivering sigh escaped before she could finish. "But I don't want him to die." Sniffling, she sat back.

The old faithful friend who had first belonged to Hunter looked up at her. She knew it was crazy to everyone else, but she swore this dog could speak to her heart with his eyes.

Forgive. And love.

That was the wisdom communicated in his gentle stare. Seemed like something Bennett would say. Things he *had* said with regard to Hazel's brother. No wonder this dog had adopted that man as his own too.

"You never struggle with that, do you?" Hazel swallowed and then twisted around so she could lean back on Moose's massive shoulder. "You just love your people. No matter what they do, how much they disappoint you." She swiveled her head so she could see his face again. "I don't know how to do that."

Moose nudged her with his nose. *Try.*

Hazel thought back to what the doctor had left her with: *Don't let the past lead to further regret.*

She would regret not going to see Hunter. In truth, she regretted not seeing him when he was in Bozeman, even though she had fought with all her gritty might to ignore that fact. And argued fiercely about it with Bennett.

Could she and Hunter reconcile? Could she find a way to forgive him for the things in her childhood that still haunted, for his abandoning her after Nana had died, and for nearly selling out their inherited property without her knowledge, let alone consent?

That seemed monumental. Impossible.

Then again, Bennett had forgiven her for her sneaky, selfish little stunt. That was no small thing. And it had opened the doors to something wonderful between them. He had gently reminded her of that fact when he'd nearly begged her to come see Hunter while he'd helped Bennett move in.

Hazel had refused. Because she was still so mad. And forgiving Hunter felt like letting him off the hook.

She didn't want him off the hook. But she didn't want to lose him forever either.

Try.

Was she that brave? That strong?

Sitting up, Hazel reached for the phone she'd left on the side table next to the sofa. Once that was in hand, she settled back against Moose, who sighed contentedly and laid his head down between his paws.

Bennett's number was first in her contact list, and she tapped it even while a tiny storm of panic stirred in her heart. She knew exactly what the man would prescribe. And he would insist on it.

But if she was the one to say what she knew he would want her to do, would he be proud of her? She felt sure he would, and she very much wanted it to be so. Because though she sometimes acted otherwise, what Bennett thought of her mattered more than the moon and stars.

This attachment to him—and craving for his approval—it felt . . . precarious. Hazel valued independence above all else. It gave her a sense of security to be reliant only on herself.

Bennett was ebbing that away—though certainly he didn't mean to. It was just this . . . this *need* for him, like she'd never had before. What if he let her down?

Years of hard work, of keeping herself to herself and her ideals a priority had established her life. Okay, perhaps her brother, and Mama Bulldog, and Janie might have had an occasional point—sometimes her isolated existence *was* lonely. But she had her dogs—and no, that wasn't a conciliatory claim.

Hazel *loved* her dogs.

And now she had Bennett.

I love Bennett. That still seemed like such a bizarre, outrageous thing to admit.

She held up the phone in her hand, his name on her screen along with a shot of them together. One of Bennett's muscled forearms was wrapped around her shoulders, and all of her was tucked up against him. Held secure.

Or trapped?

Oy. Why did that thought have to ruin such a sweet moment captured in a selfie? Rather than the way he'd held her, she focused on the way his head tipped against hers. Deep-blue eyes smiled warmly, and his expression was all sweet contentment. That should be what she thought of, focused on.

He loves me.

Also bizarre. Outrageously wonderful. And perhaps—because it was so entirely wild—not completely trustworthy. Was it?

Hazel tapped the tip of the phone against her head, then shook it as if that would dispel the fretting that found a way to ruin what had become the best surprise of her life. "I don't want to lose him," she muttered to herself, ending the emotional tug-of-war—for the moment. She had other things to worry about right then, real stuff happening in real time. She reset her mind back to the task at hand, tapping the Call icon.

"Hi, pretty mountain lion." Bennett spoke into her ear with the low, soft tone that sent a thrilling zip of electricity through her chest.

Hazel couldn't remember when he'd started calling her that, but she liked it. "Pretty mountain lion" was way better than "the badger lady."

"Hi, city boy." She still held on to that moniker for him—and had no idea if it bothered him. Should it? Originally, she'd meant it as an insult—he'd been a soft, spoiled pretty boy who had thought the whole world would bow to his easy smile. At least, that was what Hazel had surmised at first appraisal.

Turned out, first impressions weren't always accurate.

"Something wrong?" Bennett kept her from wandering too far afield from her purpose.

"Yes. Hunter."

Though he tried to muffle it, Bennett sighed. "Honey, you really need—"

"He's in the hospital." Hazel cut him off, not needing to hear the words to know what he was going to say. That she needed to mend the fences, build a bridge, and in all other metaphors, figure out a way to reconcile with her brother.

Silence beat out a measure before Bennett responded. "Hunter is in the hospital?"

"Yes. He got sick, really sick. Apparently his superior officer had to break into his apartment. I need to go."

"You're going? To Nevada?"

Both the shock in his tone, and the fact that he knew where Hunter was stationed when she hadn't, chafed. They shouldn't—both cases were her doing and not Bennett's fault. But the rub was there all the same.

"Yes." She huffed, aware that she kept repeating that word as if it was all she could do. "I'm going to see my brother."

Another four-count of silence lagged. Then, "I'm glad, Hazel. What can I do?"

Ah, that gentle tone. Bennett could undo her with that low, quiet voice that sank warmth into her heart. The unreasonable irritation that had momentarily taken possession of her emotions fell away, and Hazel let her true emotions carry into her voice. Even the vulnerability she very much wished wasn't there. "Come with me," she said softly. "Please?"

"Of course." Bennett didn't even hesitate.

Hazel latched on to the steadiness he'd become for her. Even so, something in her couldn't help but slap a warning label over the top of it. *Treat like spring ice, as it's likely to give way...*

Spring ice was the most dangerous, and she hated that comparison. Why couldn't she simply grasp the security Bennett offered her without all of the underlying doubt and unease unsettling her?

But there it was. The warning, the unsettling. And neither wouldn't budge.

FIVE

Hunter felt measurably better. He could think clearly, for one, which was a marked relief.

Even the few times he'd had a few too many, he couldn't remember having his thoughts so jumbled that he couldn't make sense of reality. Not like the day Lieutenant Commander Brighton had busted into his place and subsequently hauled him to the emergency room. Hunter only had a fuzzy, patchwork set of memories of that day two day ago—most of his knowledge as to how he'd ended up in the hospital attached to oxygen and a drip IV came from the doctor.

Man, he'd been out of it. How had he gotten that sick that quickly?

"It happens" was all his doctor had said and then instructed him to rest.

So he'd done. For two days solid. Hunter couldn't remember being so tired in his life, sleeping basically around the clock and still feeling exhausted.

But that late morning, he felt better, and he was glad for it.

A nurse came in with a tray of food just as he sat up using the remote on the bed.

"Look at you, with your eyeballs open." She smiled while she wheeled the narrow table thing in front of him. "That's a good sign."

"I feel like I might live."

"Also good." She settled the tray on the table, then checked the vitals on the machine beeping next to his bed. Next, she took his temp with a digital thermometer. "Much better numbers today too." She stepped back, folding her arms. "I'd say you're on the upswing."

Hunter sipped the orange juice she'd uncapped for him and nodded. "Good enough to go home?"

"I doubt the doctor will sign off on that. This virus is pretty nasty, and you came to us in rough shape. But you can talk to him about it when he rounds." She wiped the last set of numbers on his white board, as well as the name *Max*, which must have been the night-shift nurse, and wrote down his new numbers and her name. *Elise.*

"Elise."

"Yep. That's me." She turned with a closed-lip smile.

"Have I had you yet this visit?"

"On the first day."

"Hmm. I don't remember."

She nodded. "Not surprising. Like I said, you were in pretty rough shape. It's good to see you on the rebound."

Having sipped some more juice, Hunter set down his glass and dug around in his mind for any scrap of recall regarding this woman. None. Man, that was so weird. As insurance against the feeling of more blank spots in his mind, he studied her. Slim build, average height. Medium-brown hair and bright-blue eyes. Pretty smile. Elise the nurse was attractive.

As often did happen when confronted with a pretty blue-eyed woman, Hunter involuntarily thought about Janie. He shut his eyes against the intrusive memories that refused to budge, and the beep-beep-beep of his heart monitor jumped to a galloping pace.

Nurse Elise moved to his side, her fingers slipping against his wrist to physically check his heart rate. "You okay?"

He forced himself to look at her and nod. "Just a . . ." What? There was no way Hunter would tell this woman what had really triggered that spike. That she looked like a woman he'd once hoped to hold for the rest of his life, and her blue eyes had driven a spike of painful regret into his chest.

Nope. Not gonna say that. "A dizzy spell. It passed." Yeah. It usually did—this spell of sorts. As long as he replaced the squeeze of longing that ached with a patch of bitterness. *She was the one who ended it—and it was better that she did it then rather than later.*

He'd known plenty of servicemen who'd opened *Dear John* letters—and a fair share of those from *wives*, not just girlfriends. Those were always the worst. He'd been spared the worst.

That was what he kept telling himself.

"Maybe some food will do you some good. You really haven't eaten much."

Hunter nodded, willing to agree to almost any excuse, and wishing for the millionth time that Janie would simply vanish from his memory.

As he unrolled the set of silverware from the thin napkin, a knock sounded at his door. Expecting to see Brighton in uniform, Hunter lifted his attention from the tray to the doorway. He froze, hand in midair, when his eyes met hers.

No, not the blue eyes that persisted in tormenting him. But at the moment, mossy-green ones. Hunter had often had that very shade of green turned his way over the years. Bright and full of fire. That color indicated that Hazel was upset. Just as she had been the last time he'd seen her over six months before—when his little sister had declared that "he was dead to her," right before she'd pushed passed him from the jail cell and out to her freedom.

Why did the women in his life always get to just walk away? Free as a bird, no looking back. Why couldn't he pull that off?

He had no reason to believe Hazel had been anything but dead serious in her *dead to me* claim, and the girl was uncompromisingly stubborn. Given she hadn't even bothered to show up in Bozeman when he'd flown in to help *her* boyfriend, he was certain she hadn't relented. In truth, he had mourned the fact that she likely would never speak to him again. That made two women of deep significance in his life lost.

But she was there. Wasn't she?

Hunter blinked. Yes. Still there, and with company. Hand on her shoulder, Bennett Crofton stood at her back. He gave Hunter a weak smile by way of greeting. More than his sister had for him.

But she *was* there. Hunter took a sip of hope from that fact. Right up until she opened her sharp mouth.

"You're not dead." Hazel's expression was unreadable, which was not unusual. Hazel had always been a tough read.

Even so, Hunter expected more from his little sister. He shouldn't have, but blast it all, he did. *Forever the hopeful idiot.*

With an arched brow, he met her green-eyed glare. "Were you hoping to find me otherwise?"

Hazel winced, the movement of her brow slight. If Hunter hadn't been watching her—or if he hadn't grown up with her subtle tells—he would've missed it entirely. Her mouth flattened, and she stared at him. Disapproval rang loud and clear through her silence.

The man standing behind her, his hand still on her shoulder, cleared his throat, clearly trying to break the ice between the siblings. "Of course not, Hunter." Bennett gave Hazel a little nudge, and the pair of them entered the room. "Your sister was worried enough about you to leave Elk Canyon."

His hard blue stare was meant to chide Hunter, and it worked. Which was . . . irritating. Especially since it seemed more than likely that Bennett had talked Hazel into coming.

Rather than sink under Bennett's silent plea to try civility, Hunter shifted his attention solely on his sister. "Welcome to the land of other people. How's that going for you?"

"How do you think?"

Man, she could make a bear take cover with her stone-cold tone. He shook his head. "Hopefully, better with Bennett than it would have been on your own. You need to walk around with a warning label, Hazel."

Another cleared throat broke into the hostile banter, this time from Nurse Elise. "Are you family?" She took in the visitors, her expression wary and disapproving at the same time.

Hunter hoped she was wearing some armor somewhere under those scrubs, because who knew how the wild beast that was his little sister would react in captivity.

Worried about whatever Hazel might say next, Hunter answered the question. "This is my sister. She's charming. Don't get too close—she actually has quills."

Elise rolled her lips inward, glanced first at Hazel, then up to Bennet—who looked caught and deeply uncomfortable—and then back to Hunter. "Perhaps a visit later would be best?"

"No, I'm fine." Hunter summoned half a grin, sipped his orange juice, then looked back to Hazel. "She's just a scrap of a girl, after all. And I grew up with her salty lip." He paused while Hazel's scowl deepened. Hunter let that small grin grow, and he winked. "I've kind of missed it, to tell the truth."

Ah, that did it. Hazel dropped her glare, her hands twisting nervously in front her belly. Though she was a master at masking her emotions, Hunter caught the tightening of her jaw.

She felt bad. Guilty.

Well, she should, the little snippet. After all, who had looked after her every single day after their parents' accident? He did, that was who. Who had made sure she had clients enough to make ends meet?

He did. Who had gone back to the place that haunted his soul to make sure she was okay?

He did. And she had no idea how much any of that had cost him.

Six months of the cold shoulder. Good grief. About time she grew up.

The nurse gave Hunter's visitors one more once-over, then nodded. "If you're sure?"

"I'm sure. Thanks though."

"Doctor will round in about an hour."

"Looking forward to meeting him, now that I'm not delirious."

That earned him a smile. She finished her notations on the white board and strode toward the door. With a half a glance—one that looked intimidated—she acknowledged Hazel and Bennett and then left the room.

The door clicked shut, and the space grew silent. So, so, silent. Tension wound tight as Hazel refused to look at him, and he didn't know what to say.

Taking her by the hand, Bennett led Hazel to Hunter's bedside. "I think you two need some time."

Hazel shot a panicked look up at her boyfriend. Bennett's head moved with a subtle *no*, then he kissed her temple. "It's good to see you're okay, Hunter." He started toward the door, then paused. "Be nice."

It was unclear if he was addressing Hazel or himself. Maybe both? Either way, Bennett clearly wasn't up for refereeing, as he took himself out of the room.

And then it was just the two of them. As it had been so often when they were growing up. Something hard and painful moved in Hunter's chest—a ball of emotions so mixed and varied Hunter couldn't identify them all.

"I'm glad you're not dead," Hazel muttered. She dared a meek glance up at him.

Hunter smirked. "Did Bennett have to drag you kicking and screaming down here?"

Spine locking straight, Hazel's chin came up, and she squinted daggers his way. "No. I asked him to come with me. It was my idea."

A softness eased that tangle of emotions. Hunter's smirk relaxed into something more genuine. "Thank you." The fingers of his hand nearest her twitched, and he nearly reached to brush her hand. Nearly.

But they had a long way to go before she wasn't likely to smack his hand away and storm out of the room.

"Doctor said you were in bad shape."

Hunter drew in a long breath, the oxygen tube making his nose burn and the act of trying to fill his lungs causing a tight pinch in his chest. "I guess. I don't remember much, other than on Sunday I felt like I'd been hit by a train. Sometime Tuesday my commanding officer busted into my apartment because he couldn't get ahold of me."

"That's what I was told. You were that out of it?"

"Yeah. I don't remember a whole lot. Just that my chest really hurt, and I couldn't make sense of the lights and sounds around me."

"You'll be okay though. Right?" The tightness in her voice was telling.

At least, Hunter took it that way. He dared to reach for her hand. "I'm still here to be a pain in your backside."

Hazel squared her gaze on him—a mix of green and brown—and squeezed his hand. Her jaw locked tight, her brows knitted tight, and she didn't speak another word.

But she was there, and Hunter knew exactly how big of a deal that was.

Monumental.

Sitting at her bedroom window watching the sun paint an evening masterpiece over the western hills, Janie chewed on her bottom lip while she squeezed the phone in her hand. She desperately wanted to text Hazel. Her mind turned wildly to know how Hunter was. Though she didn't do so with a willing spirit, she prayed he was okay.

But she didn't want any of that revealed. She didn't even want to admit it. Not to herself, and particularly not to Hunter. Not that she thought Hazel would betray her. But even the slightest risk of it was too much.

Pinching her eyes shut, she drew a long, controlled breath. *I'm over it. He's over it. Waaayyyy over it. We can't even speak two sentences without making each other mad . . .*

Yeah. Their last text discussion was easy proof. Exchanged over six months before, she should have deleted the thread.

She hadn't.

That might be pathetic. But right then, when her self-control was on the wobbly side of functioning, it came in handy. She tapped open her conversations and slid through until she came to *traitor* and opened the thread.

Traitor: *Tell your friend to stop acting like a petulant child.*

Janie: *My friend . . . are we talking about your sister?*

Traitor: *That's the beast. She's not answering my texts or calls. Tell her she needs to put on her big girl panties.*

Janie: *I'll do no such thing.*

Traitor: *She's being a baby.*

Janie: *You had her put in jail. What did you expect, a thank-you note?*

Traitor: *Are you kidding? What she did was incredibly stupid. She's lucky Crofton isn't pressing charges—which might be because I took it seriously. I might have saved her backside. Our backsides. Because he could have taken everything—the land, the lake, the cabin. Everything—and we wouldn't have gotten a penny. So yeah. She should be thanking me.*

Janie: **eye roll emoji* You're such a megalomaniac. And speaking of the land, what on earth? That was a low deal you had going with*

Bennett, jerk. I don't know how it's possible that you just keep getting worse. Even without the jail thing, she wouldn't be speaking to you.

Traitor: *I had my reasons.*

Janie: *That's called greed. And selfishness.*

Traitor: *It's called looking to the future. And I want to have one. There's nothing in Luna for me.*

Reading to the end, Janie's heart rate spiked. Why did that last line cut the way it did? She shouldn't care that he didn't want to come back. He was right—there was nothing in Luna for him. Certainly not her.

Janie gripped the phone with a powerful grasp and willed the sting in her chest to go away.

A low, frustrated growl rumbled from her throat as she tossed her phone toward her bed. Hunter shouldn't possess the power to crush her heart anymore. And she really shouldn't care the way she did about whether or not he was okay.

After all, he didn't care. Not about Hazel, and certainly not about her. He hadn't for five long years. Wasn't about to start now.

Six

Bennett stood outside the room in the hallway, far enough away from the door to avoid any fly projectiles that might or might not come hurtling that way. Between Hazel and Hunter, who knew who would throw the first . . . whatever. Bennett's money was on Hazel though.

That might be an exaggeration. Bennett rubbed his temples, distinctly remembering the way they'd throbbed when he'd first remembered who he was and what exactly had happened when he'd fallen on the banks of the river. Then again, it might not be possible to exaggerate his girlfriend's fire when provoked. And Hunter was a lifetime expert at that.

Muted white light made the passage well lit but not too bright, and the smell of lemony disinfectant and sterile gloves mingled with the undertones of eggs and toast. Bennett suppressed a chuckle—because yes, though Hazel could frustrate him like no one else, she also kept him guessing. If he'd never met the little firecracker of a woman, he'd have never known how much he actually found that attractive.

Why, he couldn't say.

Shoving his hands into his pockets, he leaned back against the cool wall and shut his eyes. He was tired. From the twelve-hour drive and from the tension that rode with them. He'd been proud of Hazel for wanting to do this—to come down and make sure her brother was okay—and he'd told her so. Even with that, however, she'd been as wound up as a cornered raccoon, and he knew from experience a cornered raccoon could cause all kinds of ruckus. Hazel's silence as they'd neared their destination had been punctuated with a tight jaw and easily triggered snap.

For example, before they'd gone in to see Hunter, Bennett had stated his reservations about being a participant in the Wallace sibling reunion.

"Maybe you need to go in there alone. That way Hunter would appreciate that you did this and not assume I made you."

She'd scowled. "So you rode all this way with me to be useless?"

As that recent not-so-awesome exchange (one, in fact, Bennett had not and still did not find amusing) played through his mind, Bennett ran a hand through his hair—which needed a good trim—and sighed. There was little doubt in his mind that he'd get a sharp whack—something like "thanks for being useless back there"—and then an extended round of silence after they left the hospital.

Hazel was at her prickliest when she was uncomfortable and stressed.

Maybe it had been the coward's way out, leaving Hazel and Hunter alone to battle out their differences within moments of their first face-to-face in way too long. Then again, maybe it really was wisdom.

Bennett had been in between the two strong-willed Wallace siblings from the beginning. Hunter had apologized like a man afraid of a lawsuit (because probably he was) and had made sure Hazel understood how stupid, not to mention illegal, her stunt with amnesia-Bennett had been. For a minute Bennett had appreciated that. But then he'd started missing Hazel as he'd settled back into his old life in Chicago. And had also suffered a bout of guilt, knowing that he'd sort of asked for what he'd gotten. He and Hunter had hashed up a pretty rotten deal, and Hazel had been on the stinky end of it.

He hadn't known when he started dating Hazel for real that she had some kind of vise grip on mad when it came to her older brother, and she wasn't about to forgive him for the stunt or the jail time—even if that was all of a day and a half. And since Bennett had been in the middle of the whole situation, that was where he stayed. Right between the warring Wallaces.

He'd rather not be, because the truth of it was that he liked Hunter, and he saw where the man had been coming from when he'd first enacted the *sell their inheritance* scheme. Hunter had wanted a future—for himself and his reclusive sister—and he honestly hadn't seen one that looked hopeful or healthy for either of them at Elk Canyon. Truly, it hadn't been all selfishness that had prodded Hunter—something that continued to become plainer the more Bennett conversed with his friend.

But he understood Hazel's point of view as well. She felt abandoned and betrayed, and the setup Hunter had put into motion *had* been pretty lousy, even if the intent wasn't entirely wrong.

The Wallace siblings just needed to have a conversation. To have it out and to see that both of them cared about the other. And maybe loosen up the strings on their stubborn pride.

"Is Hunter Wallace awake?" A deep and dignified voice stole Bennett's attention. A man stood at the nurse's station a dozen feet away. His posture was severe, and he was dressed in perfectly pressed service khakis, his cap tucked smartly beneath his left arm.

"He has some visitors, Commander Brighton."

The military man nodded once. "His sister came then?"

"I believe so. She had a man with her." Hunter's nurse gestured toward Bennett.

Bennett drew himself off the wall and ironed his posture as the military man pivoted toward him. Dressed in a pair of dark-wash jeans and a Chicago Cubs hoodie, Bennett felt himself small and lacking in the presence of what appeared to be a navy officer. Swallowing back the balloon of inadequacy, Bennett stuck his hand forward to meet the man striding his direction. "Bennett Crofton, Commander Brighton."

"*Lieutenant* Commander, and that isn't necessary. John will do just fine. I'm glad to meet you. Are you family?"

"No, sir. Hazel—Hunter's sister—is my girlfriend. She asked me to drive down here with her. It's a long trip."

John Brighton dipped one nod. "I remember Hunter saying as much the last time he made it just a few weeks back."

"Right." Bennett tapped into his business decorum—the persona he used when negotiating a contract to buy his next big investment. Impassive and direct. Which likely came off as cool and a touch arrogant. "He came to help me move."

Brighton rubbed his jaw, then took his cap from beneath his left arm. Though his posture remained clearly military, his expression relaxed. "I'm glad you came—you and Hunter's sister. I sort of had the impression that would not happen."

Bennett wanted to feign surprise—and part of him was truly surprised. How much did Hunter's commanding officer know about his personal life? Seemed like that sort of working relationship would not invite a more personal connection. But Bennett had never been military, so what did he know?

"I'd like to wait, to visit Wallace. Would you mind?"

Bennett blinked at the humility of the question. "Of course not."

"Perhaps you'd walk with me, and we can grab a cup of coffee in the interim?"

"Coffee would be good." No falsehood there. He and Hazel had driven straight through, stopping only to get fuel. Movement and caffeine could only help his heavy head and stiff limbs.

Brighton gestured down the hall. "There's a cafeteria on the other side of the hospital. The food is decent, if you're hungry. My treat."

"That's thoughtful, sir." Bennett fell into step beside him, his aloof persona fading fast.

A slight upward tip at the corners of his mouth made Brighton seem even less mechanical. "*Sir* isn't necessary, Bennett. Ignore the uniform."

"I'm not sure that's possible."

He chuckled. "It took Hunter months to lose the formality when he was in my home."

Ah, so John Brighton was a friend, not just an overseer. Bennett warmed to the man even more. "Is he there often?"

"Most Sunday afternoons, the past four or five months."

"That's generous of you. I'm sure he appreciates it." Bennett appreciated it on Hunter's behalf. Having seen the marks of loneliness in Hunter's life, now more so than before he'd started dating Hazel, he was grateful John extended friendship. Though that seemed out of bounds in the military.

Yet again, Bennett didn't know the rules.

Brighton's response to that was unreadable. They reached the glass doors marked *cafeteria*, and the man held open the passage so that Bennett could go through. The next few minutes were spent ordering a plate of eggs, bacon, biscuits, and fried apples for Bennett, and a cup of coffee for the both of them. As he'd offered, Brighton paid for the whole lot.

At the older man's direction, Bennett slid onto a bench at a booth table, and Brighton sat across from him. Both hands on his paper cup, he pinned one short look on Bennett's face. "Would you mind if I said a short prayer, Mr. Crofton?"

"Bennett." A keen sense of unity clamped into place as Bennett nodded, and he felt less alone in the middle of a mess than he had a few minutes before. "And no. I think a prayer would be a good idea. Would you be sure to include one for Hunter and Hazel? They . . . they haven't been on speaking terms for a while."

Hazel would be angry with him for divulging too much. But she wasn't there. And Brighton was a praying man who had invested in Hunter. That meant a lot.

Lips pressed into a line, Brighton nodded rather than asking for specifics and then bowed his head. "Lord in heaven, I want to thank You for coffee and eggs and this young man sitting across from me. We ask for Your blessing on the food. We seek Your wisdom in our conversation. And we pray for the pair of siblings who have found that relationships can be challenging. Heal their rift, as You continue to heal Hunter's body. In Jesus's name, and for Your glory alone, we ask these things. Amen."

"Amen." Bennett lifted his head and matched Brighton's look. "Thank you."

With a thoughtful pause, Brighton sipped his coffee. "You are acquainted with God."

"I am." Bennett set down his mug but kept his hand wrapped around the warmth. "I am a Christian. I assume you are as well."

With a lightness in his eyes, Brighton nodded. "Since college. That's been near twenty-five years now. You?"

"I grew up as a Christian. My dad"—Bennett drew in a sharp breath—"he used to be a pastor. When I was a kid." Clearing his throat, Bennett leaned back and crossed his arms. He didn't really want to go into his dad. Why had he even brought him up? Better just focus on himself. "But I spent most of my adult life living like I wasn't one. I had an accident last fall—I hit my head and couldn't remember anything for about a week—and that shook me."

"It brought you back to Christ?"

"Yeah. It really did. It was like when I remembered everything again, I suddenly saw myself clearly—who I was. I didn't like it."

With the back of his knuckles, Brighton rubbed his jaw. "Sounds like an interesting story."

"It's a developing story, if you want to know the truth."

"Most are." Brighton chuckled.

The phone vibrated in Bennett's hoodie pocket. He pulled it out, and Hazel's name flashed.

Where are you?

With a small wave of the phone in his hand, Bennett spoke. "Looks like the Wallace family reunion has wrapped up."

"Do you suppose it went well?"

Bennett let one brow cock upward. "Do you want an honest answer?"

Brighton chuckled again. "Suppose I go down to say hi—I can introduce myself to Hazel. That way you can finish your breakfast."

Hazel would not love that. At all.

"I'm quite good at diplomacy." Brighton apparently read Bennett's hesitation with precision.

"Not sure you've ever met a force like Hazel Wallace."

The man laughed softly. "If she's much like her brother, then I can imagine." He bumped Bennett's fist. "Eat your breakfast, young man. I sense that you need all the strength you can get for the next few days." Then he slipped from the booth, coffee in hand, and strode away.

Though a knot of apprehension wound in his stomach, because for sure Hazel would not appreciate this, Bennett breathed out a grateful sigh.

God had sent help. Certainly Lieutenant Commander John Brighton was right there on assignment.

Seven

Hazel hated crying. In general she refused to allow herself to give in to it, no matter how strong the emotion might be. If she could help it, and she usually could—because she was extraordinarily stubborn—she wasn't about to give in to tears.

Standing there in Hunter's hospital room with her big brother looking sallow and leaning heavily back against the raised mattress, she felt that urge she despised. But she didn't give her burning tears leave to fall. It helped that Hunter, though lying there sick, gazed at her with a familiar demanding blaze in his eyes.

Might have something to do with the way she'd entered.

She hadn't meant to sound so snippy. She hadn't meant for her comment about Hunter still being alive to come out as an insult. Seemed that with Hunter, she just couldn't unwind. There was so much about him, and about their shared past, that tangled her emotions into unmanageable knots, bringing out the snarling beast in her. The badger lady.

Because that was how she handled emotions she'd rather not have.

"So Bennett dragged your skinny butt down here to make sure I was still alive, huh?"

Though Hunter spoke with a tight voice, Hazel suspected there was hurt mixed up in his words.

A pain she'd put there intentionally because she'd ignored him for six months. *He deserved that.*

He. Did.

Hazel redirected her thoughts to the conversation at hand. Stepping closer to his bed, she crossed her arms. "No, that's not true at all. It was my idea. *I* asked Bennett to come down here with me."

"He's your new emotional-support dog, hmm?"

She scowled at his stupid smirk. "Yeah. That's how things are."

"I'd sure like to know how you bewitched the man you'd tricked into believing that he'd *married you* into staying with you even after he found out what you'd done." Hunter blew out a little laugh, shaking his head.

"I didn't bewitch him." And why did Hunter have to say *married you* as if that was the most ridiculous thing a man in his right mind would ever do? Maybe men liked her kind of wild, even if Hunter didn't get it. After all, Jeremy had, hadn't he?

Hunter held a long stare on her, the amusement in his eyes softening the hardness that had been there moments before. "At least I know you still care about me, little sister."

"It'd be nice to know that it went both ways." Hazel tightened the arms she'd wrapped over her chest.

Both amusement and anger faded from his face, leaving a shadow of injury as he sat forward. "I did what I did *because* I care, Hazel.

I don't know why you're so stubborn about hearing that. Why you can't try to understand."

"You tried to sell off our land, our inheritance, without telling me, and you thought that was for my good? It's still *my* home, dang it."

Hunter dropped back against the pillows and blew out a frustrated sigh. "Yes. That's exactly what I thought. We've been over this a hundred times. You live up there like you're the only person on this planet. It's not good for you!"

Rolling her eyes, Hazel let her arms fall to her sides. "Well, I have good news for you then, brother. I have Bennett now, so stop worrying. Stop trying to sell the only thing that matters to me—the only thing that's been consistent in my life. If you don't want Elk Canyon, that's fine. But I want it."

"Yeah, I got that loud and clear. Six months of the silent treatment made that perfectly obvious. But where does that leave me? Huh, Hazel? Have you thought about that, considered me at all?"

A knock on the partially open door interrupted their heating debate. A man who Hazel had never seen stuck his head in. "Up for a few more visitors?"

"Come in, sir." Hunter straightened his shoulders.

The man stepped into the room, and his crisp uniform proclaimed him to be military. By the ribbons and pins on his pressed khaki shirt, he was an officer. "It's good see you up, Hunter." A kind expression softened his severe stance. "You look much better than you did yesterday." Then sharp blue eyes turned to look at Hazel. "I assume this is your sister?"

As the man strode toward Hunter's bed, Bennett trailed just a few paces behind. Eyes connecting with Hazel, he passed the military gentleman and came to stand beside her. His arm curled around her shoulder. "This is Hazel."

Hazel wasn't given much time to ponder the wary tone of Bennett's voice. Was he upset with her?

"Yes, sir," Hunter said, his tone respectful and all business. "My little sister, Hazel Wallace. She drove all the way down here from

Montana to make sure I was okay. Hazel, this is Lieutenant Commander Brighton."

Hazel looked at Hunter as an uncomfortable fissure ran in her gut. That was rather formal and definitely nicer than Hunter had ever introduced her before. And her brother looked . . . embarrassed?

Was this a military thing, or was he trying to cover up that they'd been arguing and likely had been overheard?

Brighton stepped forward, a pleasantness on his face that almost contradicted the stiffness of his posture and the crispness of his military dress. He reached out a hand toward Hazel. "It's nice to meet you, Hazel. I've heard a lot about you."

He'd heard a lot about her? From Hunter? Hazel was 99 percent sure that that could not be good. She worked desperately to control the flush rising from her chest, crawling up her neck, and threatening to fill her cheeks. She couldn't help but clear her throat. "It's nice to meet you too." She sounded . . . sweet. She never sounded sweet. It wasn't who she was.

Irritated at herself for acting small, Hazel added iron to her spine and tensed her shoulders, matching Brighton's posture.

Bennett, with his hand on her shoulder, rubbed small circles into her tight muscle with his thumb. Clearly he sensed her keen discomfort. Though Hazel wanted to lean into Bennett's side and accept the shelter he offered, she fought against it.

She wasn't a weak woman. She didn't need a shelter. She hadn't needed Hunter to be that shelter, nor did she need Bennett to be her refuge.

Brighton moved closer the Hunter's bedside. Hopefully ignorant of the underlying conflict in the room, he laid a kind hand against her brother's arm. "Are you feeling better?"

"Yes, sir." Hunter nodded. "I'm certainly on the mend. Although the nurse says that I won't be off oxygen anytime soon. Something about O2 sats still being too low."

Brighton removed his hand and clasped both behind his back. "Best to listen to that, I think. Don't you worry about anything on base. I've arranged medical leave for you. Rest and recover. That's all you need to do right now."

Hazel watched while a subtle storm of emotions washed over Hunter's expression. He was humbled, embarrassed. But grateful to this officer who was looking out for him. There was a tell of admiration, and perhaps even attachment, to the man nearly old enough to be his father.

Was Brighton his commanding officer? It seemed likely—wasn't that who the doctor had told her had brought him in? And the respectful air between them seemed to confirm that working relationship.

But there was more too. Something personal.

For reasons Hazel couldn't identify, a pulse of jealousy throbbed through her heart.

Hunter had always been better with people. A gift to him and a curse to her, because it meant he could not comprehend that people puzzled her, made her feel like an intruder, and she'd rather not feel small and awkward.

Bennett slipped closer, his arm around her tightening. Had he felt her wince at the sting of envy? Or sensed that she felt odd and left out?

This time she did press into his side, accepting the quiet offer of refuge.

Mr.—Commander?—Brighton returned his attention to her and Bennett. "I assume you will be here for a few days at least?"

"We will," Bennett said with ease.

Why did everyone else on the planet possess the ability to do that—to converse with ease?

"Have you a place?"

"Yes." Hazel tried to enter into the grown-up, normal conversation. Her heart raced as if she'd run up the trail to the falls. What was wrong with her that she couldn't just talk to another human? She swallowed and kept going. "We have a room at the hotel across the street."

Brighton shook his head. "We can do better than that. My kids are both in college, and their rooms are empty and available. Come stay with my wife and me for as long as you need."

Panic zipped through her body. Stay with strangers? Not on . . .

"Thank you, sir," Hunter said. "That's generous of you." He shifted his attention from Brighton and pinned it on Hazel. Full demand had taken over his silent look. It said *Do this. Don't argue.*

That panic stopped running circles through her limbs and looped a tight knot around her heart instead. She shook her head, when Bennett's arm slipped from her shoulder so that he could grip her hand.

"That is generous." He squeezed her fingers—a meaningful gesture, to be sure. "Are you sure?"

"Absolutely." One firm nod sealed the deal. "If you'll excuse me, I'll go call Victoria. We can finalize the details after you've finished visiting Hunter." He then turned back to her brother. "Remember—rest and recover. Those are your orders. Nothing more, nothing less."

"Yes, sir."

With a grin, Brighton turned to leave. "It's nice to meet you, Hazel. Bennett. I'll catch up with you both in a little while." Then he exited.

The room might as well have snapped and crackled with the edgy energy saturating the air. Hazel shot a glare up to Bennett, who still held her hand captive, and then turned it on Hunter. "I'm not staying in a stranger's house."

"Yes, you are," he shot back calmly.

"No, I'm—"

"Hazel." Bennett's quiet but firm voice interrupted her.

She looked back at him, and he slowly shook his head. "This isn't a hill to die on."

Hazel had no idea what he meant. In her experience, every hill was one to die on.

"Brighton is my commanding officer and a good man," Hunter said. "His offer was genuine and kind, and you're not going to insult him, or embarrass me, by stubbornly turning it down in favor of the one-star hustle across the road."

"That's a snobbish evaluation. Just because the place is old and a little rundown doesn't make it—"

"I live here, Hazel. I know what goes on and where it goes down. You're not staying there, and that's the end of it."

"I'm not staying at the Brighton's."

Hunter's brow lifted with a challenge. "Then you'd better start back for Montana."

She might just do that . . .

Bennett heaved an exasperated sigh. "Is it always this way with you two?"

"Yes," Hazel spat, glaring at her bother. "Hunter is always overbearing."

"And you're always stubborn to the point of stupidity," Hunter shot back.

"Glad I get to witness you both at your best." Bennett started for the door.

"Where are you going?"

"To find Brighton." He stopped just short of opening the door and making his escape. "You can stay in the questionable one-star hustle if you want, Hazel. I'll be at the Brightons'." Then he pressed the handle and tugged the door open—maybe with too much gusto. With a few long strides, he was gone.

The door clicked shut again. And her brother chuckled.

Hazel met his entertained look with a hard scowl. Didn't make one bit of difference. With Hunter, it never had.

"I guess you're right. You didn't entirely bewitch Crofton after all." He laughed again. "I'd say, little sister, you have met your match."

It wasn't funny. Hazel was not one bit amused. She marched toward the door while Hunter continued to chuckle.

"Enjoy the Brightons' hospitality, Hazel. And don't make me look bad."

She let the words hit her back as she left his room.

"Don't cancel the reservation. I'm *not* going to the Brightons'."

Sometimes this woman made Bennett want to howl. Shifting his weight, he leaned down to speak quietly to the little thing he'd once named *the badger lady*. Sometimes he remembered perfectly why. "After some investigation, I'm going to go with Hunter here. The hotel isn't an option."

Hazel rolled her fingers into fists and didn't flinch, even if he did lean into her space a little too far. "There has got to be more than one hotel in this town."

And then . . . then the harsh veneer of her mulish tendencies fell, allowing him to glimpse the reality behind it. Ah, there she was—the frightened little thing who really just needed a shelter.

"Bennett, I do not want to stay with strangers."

Bennett's heart shrank and went mushy. It was tempting to give in to Hazel's rare vulnerability. But not on this. Hunter was right—sometimes Hazel was simply blind to what she actually needed. And sometimes she was blind to the needs of others.

Wasn't everyone?

With gentle hands, he gripped her slight shoulders. "It's done, hon. I told John we were coming, and that's the end of it. His wife, Victoria, is already shopping for supper, and it sounds like she's excited to have us."

That earned him a fierce scowl. "No, it isn't done. People can change their minds."

He shook his head, leaned down, and kissed her temple. "Stop this now," he whispered. "You're the fiercest woman I've ever met. Tougher than most men and brave enough to face an angry moose for a stupid city boy. You're not the kind of girl who gives in to fear."

With his hands still on her shoulders, he felt her shuddering exhale.

"Moose aren't as scary as strangers."

"Hunter respects them. Trusts them. And he feels like it will reflect poorly on him if we refuse their hospitality. I spent a little time with the lieutenant commander this morning. I think he's a good man. A . . . a godly man." Bennett wasn't sure what kind of impact that last part would have with Hazel. He'd tried to share his faith with her several times over the past months. At most she would offer him a tepid smile and say something like *I'm glad you have something to help you deal with the past.*

Not at all a promising interest. This was a precarious relationship . . .

Even with such a thought disrupting his peace, Bennett pulled Hazel in close and wrapped her in a protective embrace.

"I'm awkward, Bennett. People think I'm . . . that I belong in a zoo or something."

"No one thinks that." He chuckled as he rubbed her back. "You haven't given them the chance to think anything about you."

"You thought that."

Bennett whispered near her ear, "That is certainly not *all* I thought." Then he kissed her jaw. "And that is most definitely *not* what I think now."

She leaned back. "What do you think now?"

With his fingertips, he smoothed back the honey-blond tresses that had slipped over her cheek. "I think that you are as smart as you are stubborn, as capable as you are independent. That you are as beautiful as you are wild, and in this instance, you are as scared as you are mad."

She frowned at his final assessment.

Bennett kissed the lines of her furrowed brow. "And I think that I love you, my stubborn, wild woman. Even when you are exasperating. And afraid."

Sighing, she fisted his hoodie and pressed her head into his chest. "I am afraid."

"I know." He regathered her and held her securely. "But do this scared. For your brother—and, Hazel?"

She peeked up at him.

"For yourself. It's time you realize that you aren't what you've always thought. You're so much more."

More than the broken girl no one wanted. The one who was always abandoned, so why bother trying to make connections? Hazel would never say that about herself, but Bennett knew the truth. He'd seen it.

That was exactly what she believed.

As she tucked in close, burying her face against him, he shut his eyes and prayed for God to break down all the lies she had believed. About herself, her brother, and about the One who could heal her very soul.

Eight

Hazel stared at the Brightons' house through the windshield, still buckled, though Bennett had turned his Bronco off several moments before. Her heart raced, the violent squeeze of each beat hot, and her belly roiled with sour lava.

Bennett's large, warm hand covered hers and squeezed. "They're just people."

She blinked. The two-story gray brick house remained solid in her view. It looked like a mansion. All huge and crisp and beautiful.

EIGHT

Hazel Wallace certainly did not belong in a mansion. She didn't belong anywhere near there.

The burn in her stomach tossed again as a faint memory of a big house, strange people, and an unwanted removal from her lakeside cabin home flashed through her mind. She'd been young, just a small girl of twelve. All alone. And terrified.

"I don't want to do this." Setting her jaw firmly, she forced back the emotion she didn't like and pulled up the firm stubbornness instead. "Bennett, I do *not* want to stay with strangers in a pretentious house. Take me to the hotel. Now."

For a moment Bennett studied her as if she were a new species. Puzzlement and a yearning to understand what didn't make sense lined his brow and bled into his blue eyes. Then the curiosity eased, and, though his compassion remained fast, he shook his head with equal stubbornness to hers. "No. We're staying with the Brightons'. And we've already been over this. John and I sat and talked for a while, and I believe him to be a good man. A kind one. So does Hunter. Don't embarrass your brother by being stubborn. And"—he lifted his hand from hers to run the back of his knuckles down the side of her cheek—"stop selling yourself short. You handle strangers just fine at your place. Men you don't know. You will be just fine here. Who knows?" He winked, grabbed her hand again, and kissed the back of it. "You might even find out that you can make new friends."

Right. Easy-peasy. "I have my Bowie and my Remington up at the cabin," she snapped. Not to mention the whole wild outdoors, in which most would be completely lost, that she knew by heart.

Bennett simply exited the vehicle.

Hazel scowled at her boyfriend's back as he stretched beside his Bronco. She wasn't looking for new friends, thank you very much. Her life was just fine the way it was. Simple. Quiet. Under control.

Sometimes she wondered why she had ever let Janie talk her into going to Chicago. Talk about outside of her wheelhouse. She could have stayed at her remote lake, kept her life within its safe boundaries—as it had been before Bennett Crofton had melted her with his twist-her-belly-up grin and too-beautiful eyes—and she wouldn't be forced to do things she didn't want to do.

Like meet people.

But then she wouldn't know the thrill of Bennett's touch. The warm security of his arms around her. The mind-numbing pleasure of his kisses. Most of all, the wonder of his love. A thing she'd never imagined possible.

No, she'd do it again if given the opportunity. Even if it meant she'd wind up here. Being forced to meet people.

With a sharp whistle, Bennett snagged her attention. He stood at the end of the driveway, near the covered front porch beside a tall Victorian-style lamp. With the lopsided grin that made her mulish resolve go mushy, he motioned for her to join him. Hazel sighed and opened the door to step out.

Her legs moved like her feet were made of iron as she slugged her way toward her still-grinning boyfriend. That tossing storm of sour heat remained a vicious thing in her stomach. Bennett's charming expression faded as she drew beside him.

He took her hand again, his voice low and serious. "I'm right here with you."

Her inhaled breath shuddered, and he pulled her into a side hug. "I promise—angry moose are way scarier."

"No. They definitely aren't. Especially when I'm armed."

"Heaven help us all if you were armed right now."

Haze scowled. "I am a *very* safe *and* legal gun owner." The collision of their opposing world views on this topic made her hold her breath.

Bennett laughed just as the front door opened. A stunning woman stepped out with a pleasant lift of her mouth. Dark-brown hair hung straight and sheened just past her shoulders, and her chocolate eyes smiled gently. "You must be Hazel, Hunter's sister."

Unexpectedly, the storm in Hazel's middle calmed as something kind and gentle extended from the woman's gaze. "I am," she squeaked.

The lovely woman shifted her attention to the man who had changed position to hold Hazel's hand again. "And is it Ben?"

"Bennett," he corrected.

Hazel felt his quick glance at her and suspected he wore a secretive, amused expression.

Sometimes Hazel still called him Ben. And he let her. Only her.

The woman at the door nodded. "Right, Bennett. I'm Victoria Brighton. Won't you both come in?"

Her hand secure in Bennett's, she followed his lead as they climbed the four steps and crossed the narrow front porch to pass through the double front door. Inside, Hazel almost gasped while she felt herself shrink to the approximate size of a gnat.

The ceilings soared above her head, the dark wood floors gleamed beneath her feet, and everything in between sheened with cleanliness and polish. The wide-open space smelled of something delicious—warm with an undertone of citrus. And the furniture—to her left a large overstuffed leather couch and love seat set with a low table in between, and to her right a long banquet-style table with high-backed chairs sat with pristine dignity. Formal.

Hazel Wallace did not belong in anything she could label pristine. Unless it was the wilderness. This was a far cry from the wilderness. Her core shook.

"Your home is lovely, Mrs. Brighton."

Bennett's smooth voice unnerved Hazel further. *He* belonged there.

Suddenly Hazel pictured Bennett at one of his high-end resorts. In her mind a fountain splashed in the middle of a perfectly symmetrical courtyard. He held a crystal stemmed glass of expensive wine and wore a dark suit that made those blue eyes dangerously gorgeous. What she saw in her imagination could be the into for that ridiculous *Bachelor* show that Janie was addicted to. And Bennett, the way-too-handsome chosen one. The man every gorgeous, though absurd, woman was vying for.

The squall in Hazel's middle stirred again. What was this man doing with her?

"Make yourself at home." Victoria breezed past that formal table and into the kitchen that overlooked the whole space. "John is changing—he just got home from work—and he'll be out shortly."

Make yourself at home? Not likely. Hazel felt like she needed to remove her footwear, for she stood on hallowed ground. She also needed a shower to remove the layers of filth that certainly she wore from a lifetime spent in a meager, dusty cabin in the mountains.

"Thanks." Still holding Hazel's hand, Bennett wandered into the depths of this shining diamond of a cavern, all steady-on and nonchalant. Of course *he* would—he fit right in.

Hazel felt like a mangy mongrel being dragged into a castle as he guided her to the island that separated the kitchen from the rest of the wide-open spaces.

"I made key-lime chicken." After applying a pair of white oven mitts, Victoria opened the oven and slid out a pan. "I hope that's okay?"

Hazel involuntarily inhaled, and then her stomach growled. Loudly.

The man beside her chuckled. "I'd say that answers your question. It smells amazing, Mrs. Brighton."

"Just Victoria." She laughed softly. "And I'm glad. It was nice to have a reason to make it. Both of our kids are off being grown-ups. When John called to say you agreed to stay with us, I was excited to have someone else to cook for."

Hazel swallowed, the enormity of her inadequacy a near-crushing weight. As if he might have a lifeline, she glanced up at Bennett. With a subtle gesture, his silent look said *try saying something nice.*

"Thank you for having us," she stammered. Her voice sounded as if she never used it—which wasn't the case at all. She talked. To her dogs. And to Bennett. Sometimes to Janie and Mama Bulldog.

If Victoria thought her to be an uncouth ruffian, which was probable, she didn't show it. Her smile remained kind, her eyes warm. "As I said, I was excited." Now at the counter that separated them, she leaned her palms against the polished buff granite and winked.

"Between you and me, just John for evenings on end gets a little tedious."

"Because I am boring." A man's voice came from behind them.

Hazel whipped around to see the man who had been in uniform at the hospital, but was now wearing jeans and a navy sweatshirt, striding toward them.

Though he wore a schooled seriousness, he could not hide the mild amusement in his eyes. "Victoria always thought that. It was the reason it took me three tries before she said yes to a date."

Bennett laughed. "How many tries before she agreed to marry you?"

"Just two." John allowed a full smile on his face as he stopped beside his wife.

"It's good to be sure." Victoria poked her husband as he dropped a possessive arm around her.

"Agreed." He looked at her as if she was *the* treasure in this big, expensive house. The one thing that mattered the most in his life.

Did Bennett look at Hazel like that? The disquiet that had been tossing within since the moment he'd parked in front of this opulent house settled as the answer came easy to her heart. *Yes, he did.*

Hazel pressed into his side and surrendered to the refuge he offered. She'd be okay. He was right there with her, and she would make it through this uncomfortable situation.

Because Bennett would see her through.

"That was delicious, dear, as usual." John Brighton patted his fit stomach as he sat back and winked at his wife.

Victoria nodded. "It was nice to have a reason to make something special."

John simply smirked at her banter and then shifted his gaze toward Bennett and Hazel. "We have Bible study this evening—not here but at a friend's house. You're both welcome to join us if you'd like."

Hazel stiffened, and she glanced at Bennett beside her. Boy, he was going to be in trouble if . . . she suppressed a growl. She could feel Bennett's interest, and a finger of resentment scraped across her heart.

Bennett had taken her to church once. She had made it clear to him after the service that the experience had been uncomfortable and she didn't want to repeat it. He had accepted that with slumped shoulders, hands tucked into his pockets, and a nod toward the ground.

The same thing had happened with Mama Bulldog a handful of times. Though that woman had been far less easy to subdue. Mama Bulldog had taken her for Easter service and a couple of Christmas Eve services. Hazel had gone because, well, because Mama Bulldog was Mama Bulldog. It took stern stuff to turn that woman down—more than even Hazel Wallace had within herself. Anyway, Hazel figured she owed MB that much. After all, the woman had taken her in more often than not. Given her a home in town during the winter so she could attend school and not be taken away by the state. Hazel was grateful.

But as far as church went, anything more than the Christmas/Easter specials, Hazel wasn't up for it. Not for the gathering of people and not for the load of guilt going to church brought in. Why did other people put up with it?

Perhaps they didn't feel the sack of unworthiness like a bag of rocks plunked on her chest the way she did. Maybe their more normal lives made it easier to ignore the sense that they lived in the shadow of a god who wasn't always fair and didn't really care who got rolled under when he wasn't looking. And because of that, maybe they didn't feel guilty for resenting said god.

Maybe it was all just her.

In any case, nothing of that situation with Mama Bulldog and the Luna Community Church applied there. With the Brightons, Hazel hadn't even wanted to be taken in for a couple of nights by this couple. She had planned on being in a hotel room, beholden to no one.

"Of course, if you don't want to join us, that's just fine. You're under no obligation. We just wanted you to know that you're welcome. If you'd rather just simply hang out here and find a movie to watch, or a game to play, or whatever while we're gone, that's perfectly understandable. Will be back around eight thirty or nine, and then I'm guessing we'll dig in to that cheesecake that Victoria made this afternoon."

Victoria nodded, her eyes never losing the warm kindness they'd held since Bennett and Hazel first had arrived. "Absolutely. Feel free to make yourself at home."

Bennett gripped Hazel's hand. "Thanks. I think we'll take you up on the offer to stay. It was a long drive, and it's been a day, if you know what I mean." He added that last part as if he needed to cover up for Hazel's silent protest. As if she needed an excuse not to go.

She didn't. She just didn't want to go, that was all.

John Brighton dipped an understanding nod and stood up. "I'll show you your rooms and give you the rundown of the remote, because those things are never the same, and then Vic and I will head out of here."

Bennett and Hazel trailed him as he led them first to a room that was done in royal blues and cream and then to one in dark brown and cream.

"Pick your lot," John said, then led them to the basement.

There, they found a sprawling entertainment space, complete with a large sectional couch, a pool table off to the side of it, and a large-screen TV on the wall. John pulled a remote from a drawer in the coffee table and passed it to Hazel. "If I were you, I wouldn't surrender this."

Unexpectedly, Hazel chuckled. "I don't know how to use it. I don't even own a television."

"Here are the basics." John gave her a quick rundown. "Now you have the com. Don't surrender it, no matter what he does."

Hazel had merely a vague idea of what the man was saying, but even so, she felt . . . valued? Bolstered?

She didn't know what. Except that suddenly she liked Lieutenant Commander John Brighton.

"You both have a good evening." The commander patted a smiling Bennett on the shoulder and strode away.

Bennett waited until the sound of the man's footfalls left the stairs, then he looked at Hazel. "You've won a fan, I'd say."

"I haven't done anything." She scowled, trying to cover up the fact that John Brighton might have been the one to win a fan.

With both hands on her shoulders, and standing behind her, Bennett shook her playfully. "Come on, Zel. Admit it. You like them."

"I don't *know* them, Bennett."

He leaned down and whispered in her ear, "You want to though."

She nudged him away. "Stop that. I'm still mad about this whole thing. I could be in a hotel room where I'm not open to judgment."

"Who's judging you?" Bennett came around to stand in front of her as the front door upstairs shut.

"At the moment? You."

He crossed his arms and gave her a look that said *come on . . .*

"And the Brightons."

"What? Why would you say that?"

"Because we didn't go to that Bible study. And then there's the separate-rooms thing."

Bennett's head rolled back, and he stared at the ceiling. "You are literally looking for reasons to not like them. That's pathetic."

"Why can't we share a room? We're grown-ups."

"We're guests in their house. Can't that be a good enough reason?"

"What we do is between us."

"Right. So let's keep it that way, hmm?" Real annoyance seeped into Bennett's tone. "Their house, their standards. It's not unreasonable, and we're perfectly capable of being respectful."

Hazel felt small under his rebuke.

"Anyway, I don't think that's really the issue here."

"No?" She stared at the floor, though she knew he kept his gaze locked on her. "What is it then?"

"You're just uncomfortable. That's all."

At the softening of his tone, Hazel felt her shoulders fall.

He reached for her arm. "It's okay to feel uncomfortable. I get it. But don't decide that you don't like other people because you feel uncomfortable. And don't assume that they're judging you. Okay?"

Hazel swallowed. She hated feeling out of control. And she hated feeling vulnerable. But maybe Bennett had a point. She really didn't have a reason to dislike the Brightons. In truth, he was right—she actually had warmed to both of them. They had been kind and welcoming. Who offered strangers to stay in their gorgeous mansion of a house and then let them simply hang out there while they weren't home? Who went to the trouble of making a really delicious meal for them, including a decadent dessert that looked like it would make everyday oatmeal a disappointment from there on out?

Bennett rubbed her shoulder. "You don't have to change who you are, Hazel." He cupped her cheek and caught her eyes with his. "I love who you are. Honest. Just, give other people a chance, okay?"

Pressing her lips tight, Hazel nodded. She was rewarded with a soft kiss on her forehead.

"Now"—he employed a much lighter tone—"what are we going to watch? After all, you have the com."

"I don't know what that means."

"Command. You're in charge. Which is normal, so you should know what to do."

Hazel relaxed, and Bennett pulled her into a gentle hug. It was amazing how he managed to smooth her prickly spines.

More, it was amazing he would do so in the first place. Most men wouldn't even try.

NINE

Who knew that atrophy would hurt so much? Muscles that he'd trained with twice-daily workouts now throbbed at the prolonged lack of use.

Hunter limped around his apartment feeling four times his twenty-seven years. Three days out of the hospital and he was still wearing the oxygen tube attached to his nose and hauling around the cumbersome tank. His body ached, as if he'd run three consecutive marathons in the past week, rather than lying in a hospital bed doing absolutely nothing.

And his lungs felt tight, which was the greater of his concern.

But he was out of the hospital. That counted for something, right?

He stopped in front of his coffeemaker to pop in a pod and pressed the blue flashing button. When his Keurig finished brewing his fresh cup of decaf, Hunter took the mug and wandered his way to his recliner. With a long groan, he settled himself in and reached for the TV remote. Rather than flicking it on, however, he simply stared at the black screen. MacGyver would provide him a decent distraction—as he had all week—but Hunter let his thoughts settle on the week before.

Thank God, or whoever, that Brighton had busted into Hunter's apartment. By the time his overseeing officer had an ambulance coming, Hunter had been in bad shape. He was grateful for the interference that had saved his life.

But he was unsure about the interference that had brought Hazel to him. Not that Hunter hadn't wanted to see his little sister . . . just not like that. Not when he was weak, flat on his back, and at a keen disadvantage in their ongoing cold war.

Even so, there was a sprout of gratitude, even there.

Hunter puzzled about how Hazel had traveled all the way down to Nevada to see him. That had been shocking. And, he assumed, evidence of Bennett's influence over her. Hunter also considered the fact that she had agreed to stay with Brighton and his wife while they remained in Fallon. That was certainly not the sister he was familiar with. Hazel, the sister *he* knew, would've dug in her heels, declared herself just fine in that rat hole of a hotel across from the hospital, and done exactly as she'd pleased. Wouldn't have mattered how much Hunter would have demanded otherwise. Mostly because she was stubborn. And noncompliant.

But also because she was terrified of people. Particularly when she was tossed into an unfamiliar environment in which she couldn't grip firm control.

Considering the miracle of Hazel staying at a stranger's house led Hunter to think on the relationship that had developed between Bennett and his little sister. Sometimes, to be perfectly blunt, Hunter wondered if Bennett hadn't lost his mind. What man—what *sane* man—would actually date the woman who had tricked him into believing he'd married her when he couldn't remember a thing? That had all the marks of crazy in Hunter's opinion—especially when Hunter knew Bennett was anything but desperate when it came to female attraction. Hunter wasn't sure what to make of that.

But there was the fact that Bennett was good for Hazel. Softened his prickly sister, drew her out of her self-involved universe, and forced her to interact with the world. This past week being a prime example.

And, as Hunter had witnessed over the past few days, Hazel was happy with Bennett. Hunter would have to be blind not to see the way she looked at the man, her eyes bright and expression warm.

Just as Hunter decided that Bennett's state of mind wasn't the concern he'd made it out to be, and that Hazel's being happy with Hunter's college friend was a good thing, the cell phone he'd left somewhere out of reach rang. Setting his mug down with a hard thunk, Hunter looked around for the stray technology while a balloon of irritation about having to get up bulged in his chest.

The phone kept ringing. Where was it, dang it? Hunter wasn't usually absent-minded, and he didn't often leave things where they didn't belong. This stupid lingering brain fog . . .

He limped to the end of the kitchen counter, where the coffeemaker sat, and found his phone. After he cleared his throat so he wouldn't bark at the unidentified caller, Hunter answered. "Hunter Wallace here."

"Good morning, Hunter. This is Dr. Sharpton. Did I wake you?"

"No, sir." He cleared his throat again. "I'm up. Just having some coffee."

"It's good to hear you're up and around. I was a little concerned that I may have let you talk me into discharging you too soon. How is your chest?"

Hunter rubbed the spot in question. Still tight, and breathing in caused a sharp pain. Man, he really wanted to say he was fine. All mended and ready to get back to work.

But he was dizzy just from wandering around to find his phone. And the tight burn in his chest did not indicate *fine*.

He blew out a long, quiet breath.

"By your extended pause, I'm going to guess it's not great." Dr. Sharpton spoke into Hunter's exhale.

"Well . . . I'm not going to be running around base today, I'll admit that."

"Hmm." The older man's tone sent up several warning flags. Did the man really believe that Hunter should be fully recovered by now? Seemed a little overoptimistic. "You're sticking with the oxygen?"

"I am."

"Good." Another weighted pause. "Here's the thing, Hunter. I'm looking at your x-rays, and I am not liking what I see."

Hunter's heart sank like a hot lead ball. "Which x-rays?" *Please say the ones from my initial admitting tests . . .* He knew that was a ridiculous hope. The doctor would be studying the most recent images—the ones taken the day Hunter had talked Dr. Sharpton into discharging him.

Something Hunter had done because a stay in the hospital over five days would draw attention—and not the kind of attention he wanted.

Unease snaked in Hunter's belly even as the sharp clench in his chest struck again. "What are you saying?"

"I'm saying I don't like what I see," the doctor repeated. His tone was stern, though still undergirded with compassion. "I'm saying continue to take it easy. And . . ." He let the rest of his thoughts go on pause for a heartbeat. Long enough that Hunter could hear *prepare yourself* in the space.

". . . and I have to report my concerns."

"Report?"

"You know how this works, Wallace. I am required to share my concerns with Lieutenant Commander Brighton."

"So much for health care being private."

"You're a navy man, and I assume you are aware of the military command exception regarding HIPAA."

Hunter sighed. It hurt. "Yeah, I know. And I'm not really surprised."

Another pause extended.

"Hey, Doc?"

"Yes?"

"What exactly is your concern? Is it long term?"

"I'm afraid so, Hunter. The image I'm looking at, the damage to your lungs could be long term. I can't say for certain right now, but . . ."

"But you've seen it before."

"Yes, exactly."

"So prepare me. What's the worst?" It took discipline to keep his voice from quaking.

"It won't heal. You won't get back to standard health."

"We're talking about a medical discharge, aren't we?" Hunter's shoulders sagged as the words left his mouth. He ran a shaking hand through his hair.

What would he do then?

"That's exactly what I'm concerned about."

Hunter swallowed. That hot lead ball that had plummeted earlier sank further still. The vise around his chest gripped harder, and he wheezed on the next exhale.

"We'll give it a little more time," Dr. Sharpton said.

A paltry offer of hope.

Hunter squeezed his eyes shut as his world continued its slow crash into disaster. "How much time?"

"I'm not in charge. Ultimately the decision will be made your commanding—"

"You've seen this before. Tell me, based on your experience, how much time?"

"If I can't clear you in a couple of weeks, you'll be discharged. Honorably, but . . ."

Honorably. That was nice. Not particularly helpful.

Hunter clamped his jaw tight as he tried to imagine what his future looked like as an *honorably* medically discharged nobody. All he saw in his mind was Luna.

And Janie.

And all of the memories he despised at Elk Canyon.

Not a life he wanted. Not even for the woman he had loved.

"Hunter?"

"Yeah." He cleared his throat. "I'm here."

"I'm sorry to call you with this. But I didn't want you to be blindsided."

"Sure."

"We'll talk more when I see you again. I see you're on the schedule for Friday?"

Hunter leaned forward, leaning his forehead into his hand and propping his elbow against one knee. "Yeah, that sounds right."

"Good. We'll see how you are in four days."

"Right."

"Hang in there, Hunter. No matter what, you're still breathing. Still alive. That's a good thing."

"Right," Hunter repeated. He barely heard his own voice for the high-pitched squeal in his ears.

The doctor gave up the pep talk and said goodbye. Even after Hunter clicked End and set the phone on the side table, his ears still rung.

Life had just taken him to the mattresses. And he'd got beat.

TEN

Hunter stared at the paper in front of him, his world crashing around him.

It had been two weeks since his phone call with the doctor. Two weeks of desperately hoping—even praying to a God he did not like nor trust—for a change. Some kind of improvement in his breathing, healing in his lungs.

All to no avail.

"I tried, Hunter." Lieutenant Commander Brighton stretched forward and leaned his elbows against his desk. "Truly I did, son. But without a doctor signing off, it was a hopeless cause. There simply isn't another choice."

Hunter's gaze flexed to his commanding officer and then narrowed right back on that piece of paper. One slip of paper and his world had gone to crap. The worst had materialized. Medical discharge. An irrevocable decree. The end of his military career. What would he do now?

"Hunter, I know this feels like a low blow. But you will get through this. You're a skilled man and a hard worker. I have a lot of connections. I can help you find something in a civilian life." Brighton kept an unwavering gaze on him, concern carving deep in his brow. "Here or elsewhere. I'll help you figure this out."

Hunter heard the voice of the man sitting across from him, but Brighton's words became distant and muddled in his mind. All he could really hear, all that kept going on incessant repeat through the rushing heat in his ears, was *medical discharge... medical discharge ... medical discharge.* As if walking through the murky heaviness of a bad dream, Hunter rose slowly and turned to make his exit.

"Hunter." Urgency rang in the lieutenant commander's tone. "Come over for dinner tonight, son."

Hunter heard the authoritative command from his ranking officer, but he didn't look back. He shook his head. "Not tonight, sir. Thank you though."

"Don't try to go through the hard times alone. Nothing good will come of it. Victoria and I enjoy having you, and I'd rather not think of you sitting in that dark apartment all by yourself trying to process this."

Hunter shook his head again, and this time he looked back. He found sincere friendship holding fast onto him. "I just need some time."

Brighton nodded. "I can understand that. But just know I'm coming after you. I simply will not allow you to take this blow by yourself."

Hunter processed for three days, and Brighton left him to it for that length of time. But apparently that was the limit.

His former commanding officer pounded on the door bright and early the following Saturday morning. "Wallace. Open the door."

Dressed in his sweats and a navy hoodie, and slumped in his recliner, where he'd spent the majority of the past thirty-six hours, Hunter glared at the front door. "I'm sleeping," he muttered to himself. "Leave me alone."

He had no idea why he lied, particularly when he was the only one who could hear it.

"Hunter." A string of three more firm knocks sounded. "I'm not kidding. I've broken in before, and I'll do it again if I have to."

There was no lie in that. Hunter groaned as he leaned to kick the footstool down. He moaned as the stiff muscles in his back and legs proclaimed their inactivity while he stood.

Two more knocks.

"I'm coming," Hunter spat. Shuffling, because, wow, was he tight, he made his way through his dreary apartment to the front door. He rubbed the burn in his chest and momentarily wished he was wearing the oxygen so that breathing didn't feel so hard. With an annoyed flick, he unlocked the deadbolt and the knob, then jerked open the door.

"Good morning, sunshine." Brighton looked him up and down and frowned. "You look awful."

"It's, like, six in the morning."

"It's nine."

Hunter shoved forked fingers into his oily hair, then let his hand drop until it smacked his leg.

"Mind if I come in?"

As if he had a choice. He motioned toward the inside of his place and stepped back.

His posture ever erect, Brighton strode forward, flicking on the lights as he reached the kitchen. There, he searched the counter, inspected the garbage, and checked the fridge. "Living on Cheetos, popcorn, summer sausage, and"—he leaned to peek into the trash again—"a steady stream of beer." Arms crossed, he squared a raised-brow look onto Hunter. "Didn't you tell me that your grandfather drank himself to death?"

Hunter slouched against the wall and shrugged. "Might have."

"This is pathetic. You're an officer in the US Navy. Do better."

Pinning a glare onto the intrusive man, Hunter scowled. "Was." Dragging himself off the wall, he slinked to the fridge, jerked the door open, and grabbed another beer. "Discharged, remember?"

"Honorably." Brighton ripped the unopened can from Hunter's hand. "So be honorable." He popped the top and dumped the drink down the sink. After tossing the can, he turned his inspection back onto Hunter himself. "You looked terrible."

"So you said."

"You smell terrible too."

"Thanks."

"Go shower."

Hunter simply held the man giving orders with an impassive stare.

"Now."

"You know I don't have to take commands from you anymore, right?"

Brighton gripped Hunter's shoulders and turned him so that he faced the direction of the hall. "Shower. Use soap, for the love of dignity. Victoria has brunch planned, and then you and I are going to the gun range."

Hunter looked back at him. "Think that's a good idea?"

"Sometimes you just got to blow something up." Brighton patted his back. "But first, you can't come to my wife's table smelling like you rolled in roadkill." Then he pushed him forward.

And Hunter complied. Old habits. Or gratitude. Probably both.

A little more than an hour later, Hunter felt closer to manhood as he finished off Victoria Brighton's Mexican egg casserole, complete with a side of avocado slices and a bowl of cut pineapple. His lungs still felt tight, and again he wondered if he should have swallowed his pride and brought his breathing tube along. After all, Brighton had told him he smelled like a dead animal. Couldn't get much lower than that.

He rubbed the tight spot in his chest.

"Still bothers you, doesn't it?" Brighton said.

"What's that?"

"Breathing. It's still hard."

Hunter looked at the glass of orange juice, half-gone, sitting above his plate. He nodded. "Yes, sir."

"When do you see the doctor again?"

Still not making eye contact, Hunter shrugged. "Not sure. Supposed to in a week."

"Supposed to?"

Hunter shrugged. "Not sure I'll be here that long."

"Where will you go?"

"Home." Finally, he looked up.

Brighton met him with a concerned look. "Back to Montana?"

"Yes."

"Seemed like you hadn't any intention of going back there."

"I didn't. But things change."

"Hunter, I told you I could help you—"

Nodding, Hunter held up a hand. "I know. And I appreciate it. But right now . . ."

"Sometimes you just need to go home." Victoria reached across the table and squeezed Hunter's arm. "To your family. Your people."

Hunter wasn't sure he really had that. Yeah, he had a sister—one who barely tolerated him, and he knew exactly why. Hazel was never gonna see things the way he did. That was his own fault—and he didn't regret that one bit.

As to his people . . . Janie's lovely face, her melt-his-middle-to-pudding blue eyes, flashed through his mind. She wouldn't look at him that way anymore though. Not ever again.

He'd burned that bridge to ashes.

Home had been the last place he'd wanted to go. But now ... now it was either drink himself into the legacy his grandfather had left for him, live in the Brightons' pity—which made him feel way too much like the boy who had just watched, like a coward, while his grandmother took a beating—or go home and face the ghosts of Elk Canyon.

The ghosts were the lesser of all evils.

"How can we help?" Victoria said into the extended pause.

Hunter peeked at her and then slid his look to Brighton. *John.* He was a friend now. Swallowing, Hunter clenched the fist in his lap as he battled a surge of raw emotions. Never in his life did he think he'd ever say this . . .

"Pray for me."

It seemed like a last resort. A shot in the dark. But it was all that Hunter could think of.

John reached from the other side of the table and gripped Hunter's shoulder. "Every day, son." He dipped a firm nod. "As I have done for the past two years."

That was . . . shocking. And Hunter had no idea why it nearly brought him to tears.

A low-hanging dust cloud hovered around her legs as Hazel finished with the tack room cleanout she did every spring. She neared the door, the task nearly done, when the rumble of a vehicle on the north ridge invaded the sounds of chirping birds and the breeze rushing through the pines.

Bennett?

He hadn't said anything about coming up anytime soon. As far as Hazel knew, he was neck deep in a new contract for a flip on the west side of Bozeman. He'd sent her pictures—the house looked massive to her. Bennett had called it *dated*, but also *a diamond in the rough*. She was glad he was finding a niche there, especially because that relieved her anxiety that he would come to regret moving. And resent her for it.

I want you to trust my love...

Why did she keep replaying him telling her that? It was . . . aggravating. Or something else equally uncomfortable. She trusted his heart. Usually. Well, for the present time.

For the future? In Hazel's experience, life changed. People changed. Without notice.

The sound of brakes squeaking broke Hazel's thoughts and the yucky tightening of her gut. Leaning the broom against the open door, she brushed her dusty hands against her jeans and stepped into the brilliant late-May sunshine.

Perhaps Bennett had come up to surprise her. He was that kind of man. Thoughtful and kind. Though sometimes his teasing got old, and he was still very much a city boy, Bennett Crofton had proven himself to be nearly the opposite of the first impression he'd given her.

Much better things to set her mind on when it came to her boyfriend. An eager smile teased her lips as she walked toward the cabin. Rubbing her dusty hands against her jeans, she came round the side of the cabin and stopped dead. The grin on her face froze as the anticipation in her chest stalled.

That was not Bennett's Ford Bronco, and the man shutting the vehicle door, though familiar, was certainly *not* the man she expected.

"Hunter?"

With a posture one would expect of a navy man, Hunter turned slowly, adjusting the ball cap that covered his sandy-blond hair. When he met Hazel's stunned gaze, Hunter wrestled up half a smile. "Glad to see me, I see."

"I am," Hazel responded, too quickly. "I mean, I'm glad you're better. You are better, right?"

"As well as I'm going to get, apparently."

"What?"

Hunter kicked a stone that dared to get in front of his boot and shoved his hands into his pockets. When he lifted his face up so that Hazel could catch his eyes again, there was a stony glare in place of that fake almost-a-grin he'd attempted. "Home sweet home," he muttered, his resentful gaze moving from her to the cabin and then settling on some distant spot of the lake.

"What?" Hazel spat the word out again.

"Thrilled?" Her brother jerked his attention to her and then nodded. "I knew you would be."

"I don't know what you mean. Are you saying . . ."

"I'm back."

"What does that mean?" She said each word slowly as she closed the space between them.

Hunter pointed his unsmiling face back to the lake and stared. His jaw worked, and the tension in his shoulders made the muscles defined even through his T-shirt. "The navy and I broke up." He glanced down at her as she stopped beside him. "Medically discharged."

Her lips parted as a painful spasm gripped her heart. Discharged? But . . . but Hunter had planned to be a career seaman. It had been his escape—the one Hazel had resented him for. They couldn't just *discharge* him. He hadn't done anything wrong. Had he?

"Because you got sick?"

"Because my lungs are damaged." He rubbed his chest, then jammed his hands back into his pockets.

"But surely they'll heal."

"Doctor doesn't think so." He swallowed, the dip of his Adam's apple hard. "Asthma is not an acceptable health condition in the US Navy."

"But—"

He spun to pin his glare on her. "I've tried all the arguments already, little sister. Didn't do any good, and I have no say. So now here I am. Stuck in this pristine prison all over again. Guess you get to deal with it too, because I've got nowhere else to go. I'm sorry that's an inconvenience to your disown-your-only-family life plan, but that's just the way it is."

Every word of that hot speech cut, each sentence slicing deeper. "Hunter..."

His lips pressed together into a hard line, and he looked away, leaving her with the view of his clenched jaw. Hazel stood there staring at the big brother she had both adored and despised. Hunter's severe frown seemed out of place for the man she'd known to tease mercilessly. His scowl was more fierce than he'd ever clamped on her when she'd done something that had made him irate—like tricking an amnesiac man into believe he'd married her.

He was serious. And devastated. Pain spasmed in her chest again. "I'm sorry," she whispered.

He flinched, looked toward the hills that rose up opposite of where she stood, and then pinned his unhappy eyes back on her. "I'm sure you are." Then he pivoted from her, stalked to his truck to snatch a pair of bags from the cab, and set his march toward the cabin.

Hazel couldn't help but notice the slump of his shoulders. The military posture had faded.

Her brother had been beaten. It broke her heart.

Janie wiped the polished wooden counter with a wet cloth. The group of old men she'd tagged *The Old Man Coffee Club* had, five minutes before, left a few brown mug rings and several crumbs of her coffee cake as a testament of their one-hour solve-the-world's-problems session.

Happened every Thursday.

She came to the end of the twelve-foot bar, when the bell over the front door chimed. "Just in time for the last slice of—" Janie looked up right before she said "coffee cake," and didn't finish. "Hazel." Joy lifted the corners of her mouth. "I didn't expect to see you for at least another week." She motioned with her head for her bestie to come in and sit. "What brings you down from the lake?"

The woman at the door remained planted there. And didn't return Janie's happy grin. Instead, she wrung her hands.

"Hunter is home." Hazel dropped that bomb carefully, as if she knew it would explode in Janie's mind.

Which it did. A series of white lights flashed behind Janie's eyes as she involuntarily imagined Hunter standing in her doorway rather than Hazel. His charming half grin sliding upward, making her heart slide sideways and tummy do delightful little flips.

All dumb stuff. Because Hunter wouldn't look at Janie like that anymore. He would scowl. And Janie wouldn't melt like that anymore. She would burn.

With determination, Janie refocused her mind on *Hazel* standing at the door. Dropping info grenades. Of course Hazel would know that Hunter being in town would hit Janie like an explosion—she was Janie's best friend. And Hunter's little sister.

But did Hazel know all of it?

Janie didn't know how she possibly could. *Janie* didn't know all of it. She didn't understand what exactly had gone wrong. How had she misunderstood so badly? She thought they'd made a promise and had been convinced Hunter had been honorable.

Such was the downfall of entrusting a girl's heart to a wounded man.

"So you and Hunter have made up, have you?" Janie gave Hazel a smirk and passed off this little bit of news as if it really didn't bother her. Hunter coming back *shouldn't* bother her. After all, he'd be gone within a matter of days. Off chasing his great glorious life somewhere other than in Luna, Montana.

Without Janie reminding him of home.

Hazel squinted her eyes and shook her head. "I don't think you understand."

"Understand what?" Janie shrugged "I understand Hunter is home, and apparently his near brush with death has solved all your relational problems. The siblings are on speaking terms yet again. Good for you."

"Janie. Hunter is *home*." Hazel spoke each word slowly. Intentionally. As if Janie did not understand at all.

Wait. Did Hazel mean . . . "Hunter is . . ." Janie could barely make it through two words, let alone the rest of the implied information. Hunter was *moving* back to Luna? For good?

Nope. *Not* for good. Nothing about that could possibly be good.

"Hunter is home to stay. Janie, he was medically discharged from the navy." Hazel's steady look demanded Janie meet her gaze.

She did. Briefly. Then Janie blinked and looked away. Light and heat exploded in the back of her head, as if she'd taken a physical blow. How could she possibly survive life in tiny Luna with Hunter Wallace back in residence?

Did he think he'd just waltz back into town and pick up everything where he'd left off?

Certainly not *everything*. Even the thick-skulled man of Elk Canyon couldn't image that sort of absurdity.

But did he?

In the midst of that dizzying curiosity, Janie's mind replayed the part where Hazel had said that Hunter had been medically discharged. His naval career was over. She knew him well enough to know that had been a hard blow, and the sliver of her heart that didn't burn with residual anger at the man throbbed with a ribbon of pity.

Nope. Not feeling sorry for Hunter. That would make her way too vulnerable.

She knew that for a fact, because compassion for Hazel's complicated, wounded older brother had been what started everything in the first place. But she wasn't seventeen anymore. And she knew better than to get pity confused with other things.

Just in case, however, Janie schooled her expression and wrapped her heart within a twisted ball of barbed wire before she turned back to her waiting best friend. Meeting Hazel's concerned look, she brushed up her best, most confident smile. "We could throw him a welcome home party. Wouldn't he love that?"

"No."

Janie snorted. "Don't I know it? So much the better."

"Janie."

"I'm teasing."

"This is serious."

"I know. Are you going to be okay? I mean, you're his sister, and I assume he's moving back into the cabin, and you two haven't been exactly on the friendly side of sibling life."

"I'll be fine. I'm always fine."

"Yep. So is Hunter. I guess you two will make it out fine together." Janie knew a bitter bite underscored her tone. She couldn't help it. "Just like always, right?"

Hazel's eyes—currently bright green—lowered as her shoulders sagged. "Swear you won't let this ruin us."

Ah, there was the squeeze of pity again. This time, though, for Hazel. That was acceptable. Janie reached across the counter and covered Hazel's forearm. "Nothing ever could, Zel." She squeezed. "Not even your dumb brother."

Especially not him.

Hazel attempted a half smile. It looked more like doubt than anything else.

Eleven

Janie pulled her streusel coffee cake out of the oven, inhaling the sweet aroma of cinnamon and brown sugar. A small grin of satisfaction bowed her lips, and though she was still in a bent position, her feet did a little happy jig. She did love the quiet hours of early morning, and she always felt a keen sense of a job well done when she pulled her coffee cake fresh from the oven.

The start of a new day. The sun had broken bright and warm, washing the valley in pure white gold. A promise of hope. Janie held on to that promise, especially after she had tossed and turned last night, wrestling with Hazel's announcement.

Hunter. Home. Permanently.

What were the odds that she could avoid the man if he was going to be a lasting resident up at Elk Canyon once again? Did that mean he'd be down at Luna as often as he had been when they were teenagers?

Surely not.

Janie glanced at that mouthwatering coffee cake she'd slid onto the counter to cool. Even back when they'd been little more the children playing grown-up, Hunter had loved her coffee cake.

No. She shook her head, as if commanding the possibility to crawl back into the dark corner from whence it came. Surely Hunter wouldn't want anything to do with Luna, let alone Janie's café—cinnamon streusel coffee cake notwithstanding. Right?

Janie turned to the large carafe of coffee she'd brewed when she'd first arrived in the kitchen—round about 4:30 a.m. It was time to get a fresh pot going for the front . . . She had things to do aplenty. There was no time to dwell on would-be problems.

Yeah. Tell that to those pesky thoughts that pinged around in her head.

Her mind had already turned over and over the worries of Hunter Wallace throughout the chilly darkness of the night. And now, as he reentered her tossing cares, it became so easy to forget the gold light of that new morning and the whispered promise the new day had offered moments before.

She reached for her Bible, tucked into the far corner of her kitchen, semi-protected from wafting flour and stray splatters, to reread the morning passage. *Be anxious for nothing.*

How was it possible that within the space of two hours she had already abandoned that instruction? Perhaps it was because of her lack of practice when it came to reading her Bible.

She reread it again, whispering the words as she committed them to her heart. The tingling of the bell at the front of the café drew her away from the Bible and to the first customer of the day. With the flip of her wrist, she looked at her smartwatch: 6:45? Pretty early for a Friday. Her Bible still in hand, Janie came through the swinging door that separated her kitchen from the dining area and then stopped cold.

No! What was *he* doing there? At 6:45 on a Friday morning?

"I assume you're open." Hunter didn't stop for an answer but straddled the first barstool he came to.

Janie's stomach somersaulted, and the fluttering within felt like a million delightful bubbles bursting with excitement. An entirely unacceptable physical reaction to seeing Hunter again. She folded her arms tight across her chest, hugging her Bible, and banished all such marvelously stupid responses. He wasn't allowed to make her feel that way. Not ever again.

Rather than grinning a silly, girlish smile that the man had so easily summoned from her a million times before, Janie scowled. "Kind of early for you."

"I thought I'd catch the Old Man Coffee Club."

"You haven't grown up enough for that group." Janie plunked the Bible onto the counter, then anchored her hands on her hips. "It's unlikely you ever will. And besides, they meet on Thursday. You haven't been gone long enough to forget that."

"Things can change, even in Luna." Hunter put his gaze directly on her, forcing her to meet his eyes. A calculated move to be sure. "And I've been gone long enough."

A painful-pleasant squeeze in her chest let Janie know that her command that he *not* affect her in such way was not heeded. Blast him for that. She swallowed. With a sharp inhale, she marched across the space that separated them. "Don't even try it, Hunter Wallace. You lost all rights."

One light-brown brow lifted as he leaned forward. "Try what, Janie girl?"

"To use your charm on me. It won't work anymore. I know exactly why you're back, and it has nothing whatsoever to do with me, so save your intense stares and . . . and general manipulation."

The warm teasing in his eyes shuttered, and as he sat back, his expression turned to stone.

Regret and sympathy tried to nudge past Janie's chilly resolve. She squared her shoulders against it. "Maybe you should just move on."

"I'm a paying customer."

"Then order. And leave."

His face tilted back up, and those eyes clamped on hers again. No more teasing. No more of that rather intimate, hopeful gleam. Just irritation. "Coffee," he said, still holding that dead cold stare. "And a slice of that cinnamon coffee cake."

Desperately holding tight to the iron gate she'd closed on her heart, Janie spun away to retrieve his food. As she cut and plated a slice, she found her hands shaking, and it was then she realized how hard her pulse pounded.

Hunter needed to go. She couldn't be around him and think straight. He made her either a foolish pile of mush or blinding, ugly mad.

She returned to find him staring at the kitchen door, waiting for her. Ahem. For his food. With a careless clunk, she placed the plate and then the mug of black coffee in front of him.

In the tense silence that beat between them, she caught the lift of his chin as he inhaled the wafting smell of her cake and the passing look of appreciation that crossed his expression.

Not that it mattered.

"Surely you didn't come down from the lake just for coffee cake."

"It's good cake." Picking up the fork that had been on his plate, he focused on fixing a loaded bite. "Have you seen what Hazel keeps by way of food up at the cabin?" He shoved the food into his mouth and stifled a groan.

His obvious appreciation of her work didn't matter to Janie at all. Lots of people liked her food. That was how come her little café could survive in this tiny town.

Hunter glanced up at her, the light of humor back in his eyes. "Between you and me and all of Montana, even if she did have something decent to work with, Hazel is a terrible cook. Tell everyone."

"You could make your own food."

"I could." He took another bite. Then a sip of coffee.

And just kept eating.

She shouldn't be irritated that he didn't try to make conversation. It'd be best, in fact, if they didn't talk. She had nothing good to say to this man. But when it came to Hunter, everything he did was irritating.

Every word from his mouth was irritating. Every look from those wonderfully warm brown eyes was irritating. The way he hadn't shaved, leaving a manly, sexy shadow on his face was irritating.

His silence was irritating. She ended it. "You're not going to sulk around Luna, being useless, are you?"

"What?"

"You own a whole lake and, like, half a mountain. Certainly you can find something useful to do."

"I left Luna to do something useful."

"You left because you were too scared to stay."

His glare could have been an artic squall. "Well, now I'm here. Guess you got your way."

Her way? Not even close. Her way had been that Hunter never leave. That she never would have known the rage that came from a heart so utterly let down and broken that it might not ever hold love again.

Now, her way would be that, like the wandering soul who had been her father, Hunter would never come back. She didn't get either.

"Lucky us." Janie shook her head while the words left her tongue like the tannins from a choke cherry. "The navy gave you skills, I hope."

"The navy gave me the boot."

"So I heard." She refused the sprout of sympathy any soft place to take root. Sympathy for Hunter Wallace had gotten her nothing but a broken heart. Janie wasn't going to be twice gullible.

"Can't break free no matter how hard I try. Guess that makes you right." He smacked the mug he'd just sipped from onto the wooden counter. "Doesn't that just make you smug or what?"

"No." She crossed her arms and tried to ignore the javelin piercing her chest. Rather than feel sorry for being a snippet—right then, and in fights that had happened in years past—she smothered regret with anger. "But don't think you're going to waltz back into Luna and you and I will pick up where you let things drop. I'm not the malleable girl you took me for."

"Malleable?" Hunter dropped his fork. "I never once took you for that. Kind. Sweet. Loyal. All of those, yes, and clearly that was a mistake. But not—"

Every one of those adjectives landed like a searing jab. Janie slapped the counter and leaned in. "Let me make this real clear, Hunter. You and I are done. D-O-N-E. Done. I haven't been here waiting for you."

"I didn't imagine you were." The cake finished, he dropped his fork onto the plate and wiped his mouth with a napkin. Then he wadded it into a ball and tossed it onto the plate as well. "Bitterness sure did a number on you, Janie."

"Whose fault is that?"

He shook his head, his piercing gaze locked firmly on her. "What was it Mama Bulldog used to say? 'You can't help what other people do, but you can decide how you live.'"

"Don't quote my mother to me."

"Of course not. You already know all the right things." Pushing off the bar, he stood and strode toward the door. There he paused and shot a look over his shoulder. "It doesn't look good on you, Janie."

And then he jerked open the door and stormed out.

Blinking, Janie seethed as she tried to figure out what he meant. He was down the street before the words connected with understanding.

Bitterness. It didn't look good on her.

It sure didn't feel good either. But that was his fault, and what was she supposed to do about that?

Hunter bumped and bounced over the rough dirt road with too much pressure on the gas. A brown, dusty cloud billowed behind his pickup, and he had to press hard on the brake to make the tight left curve that would take him to the cabin. The tail of his vehicle slid right, the earth beneath his tires scattered, and if not for the slight rise on the right-hand side of the road, he would be in a full roll on the back side of the ridge.

The truck settled precariously. Hunter's heart had kicked hard, and now a rush of adrenaline zipped through his limbs.

He needed to get a grip. Before he killed himself.

Hands on the steering wheel, he squeezed his fingers into a white-knuckled fist and shut his eyes.

I haven't been here waiting for you.

As the arrow of that hissing statement sank deeper, Hunter swallowed against the fresh jolt of pain. He hadn't expected that Janie would be there waiting. Hadn't even really expected that she'd be thrilled his was home.

Why, then, had he gone down the hill to see her?

It'd been stupid. Desperate.

Yeah. Both of those in high doses, because deep down he had hoped against all reasonable odds that Janie's compassion would meet him in that tiny café, not her seething resentment.

Insane. He should have known better. He *had* known better. But he hadn't truly understood the depths of her bitterness toward him. Seeing it fresh and firsthand rather than from a distance via a few venomous texts was a new kind of agony.

Janie wasn't that girl. She hadn't been, and he couldn't believe that deep down she really was now.

She was all the things he'd said of her—kind and sweet and mostly loyal. She had been his confidant. His solace. And the love of his life. Right up until choices had to be made.

He couldn't stay. Janie had known that, hadn't she? All the secrets that had haunted him, from the time he was a boy trying to take a man's place, Janie had known. Because he'd entrusted her with them. How could she imagine that he could stay in Luna, let alone up at Elk Canyon, knowing the nightmares he'd lived through there? She *had* to have known he had to leave.

But she had refused to go with him.

Leaning forward, Hunter pressed his forehead against his knuckles while the fight that ended everything erupted in his mind.

"ROTC? Hunter, isn't that a commitment?"

"Yeah." He cupped her shoulders, confused by the tension that knotted her body and expression. *"But it's a good deal. It's our ticket out, Janie. It'll give us a good future."*

She stared at him, lips parted. "Ticket out?"

"To a new life. Out of this tiny town. It's freedom."

"I don't want out."

"What?"

She stepped back, and his hands slipped from her shoulders. "Hunter, this is my home. My mom is here. Hazel is here. We're all here, waiting for you to come home."

He reached for her hand, but she tugged free the moment his fingers curved around hers.

"We'll make a new home." His voice took on a mix of desperation and frustration.

"With the navy? Are you kidding?" Janie shook her head, stabbing him with an angry glare. "You don't have a home with the navy, Hunter. You'll get shipped to who knows where for nobody knows how long, and I'll be stuck in some strange place by myself."

"We'll figure it—"

Though a tear flicked onto her cheek, Janie shoved his chest. "How could you do this?"

"I—"

Her anger blindsided him as she erupted. "You led me to believe... Now you're just going to leave? To stay gone? What about this?" *She held up her left hand.*

On her fourth finger, she wore the simple Black Hills–gold band with a speck of a diamond held between two leaves. It had been all he could afford before he'd left for college, but that hadn't seemed to bother her. She'd said yes. Enthusiastically.

"We can get married now." He caught that hand and drew it to his lips. Then he tucked it against his chest. "Let's go. We can elope, start our own life right now. It'll be you and me against the world, and we'll make it, Janie. I swear we'll be okay. Just, not here. I can't stay here."

By then streams of tears flowed down her cheeks. "I can't believe you did this without talking to me."

"I did it to give us a start."

"You're just running away."

"Janie..."

Shaking her head again, she withdrew her hand and crossed her arms, as if to make a tight shield to keep herself from him. "I'm not leaving Luna. That wasn't what we talked about."

"We never talked about staying."

A long stretch of horrible, heartbreaking silence lengthened between them.

"I belong here," she finally whispered. "I can't leave." And then...

Janie walked away, tearing his heart straight out of his chest.

Sitting there in his truck, the engine still running and his life once again turned wrong side out, the pain of her abandonment throbbed every bit as hot and sour as it had that night. Janie hadn't gone with him back then, she hadn't been waiting for him in the in between, and she had no desire to see him now.

It all was so tragically unfair. Because in spite of her breaking his heart, the stubborn woman retained ownership of it, even if she didn't want to. And though he knew it was stupid, Hunter couldn't help but wish they could give it another go.

And that was his curse. He'd simply never be able to break free from the past—not from the things he wished would let him go and not from the hopes and dreams he wanted back.

TWELVE

After parking near a large pine and climbing from his vehicle, Bennet stretched and then sent up a brief prayer for wisdom. He always looked forward to seeing Hazel, but this weekend might be bumpy.

It would be a lot less complicated if they saw things from the same point of view.

Bennett pushed through the front door of Hazel's cabin with his backpack slung over his shoulder and a tangle of mixed emotions stirring in his heart. They needed to talk. He'd been putting it off, but his conversation with José after Bible study two days before had increased his resolve. That had been his reason for calling it a week late yesterday evening, letting his real estate agent know he'd be unavailable from Friday through Sunday, and driving from Bozeman to Luna that morning.

To his surprise, when he stepped through the front door, he found Hazel sitting on the small sofa that took up most of the small space in her tiny home, staring at her folded hands.

"Zel?" The needed conversation fled to a far space in the back of his mind. Something was wrong. Bennett let the pack slide from his shoulder and drop to the floor as he crossed the space. This wasn't normal—Hazel didn't just sit and stare. He'd not even thought she'd be inside. It was a beautiful day—the sun gently warming the high-altitude lake from its blue-sky throne. Typically, Hazel would be somewhere out in it, and he would have to hang out at the cabin until she made her way back down whatever trail she'd wandered and to the cabin.

Time he'd banked on to get the needed conversation straight in his mind and build up the resolve in his heart to have it.

Hazel's unsmiling face turned toward him. She tried to lift a corner of her mouth, but it wasn't successful. "I didn't know you were coming."

"I know." Was this directed at him? Bennett couldn't think why it would be—other than the fact that he'd roped her into staying at the Brightons' during their three days in Nevada. That'd been weeks ago though. Surely she wasn't still mad? Then again, Hazel had talons when it came to mad . . . Bennett tempered a sigh and hoped his spiraling suspicions were wrong. "I thought it'd be a surprise. Is that okay?"

"Sure. Better than the one I got yesterday."

"What was that?"

Hazel stood and walked to the window. Then she turned, and her gaze grazed over him and landed somewhere by the bedrooms at the back of the cabin. "Hunter is here."

"He is?" Bennett turned toward the back rooms, half expecting to see Hunter appear at the sound of his name. No Hunter materialized.

"He was medically discharged."

"Medically discharged?" Bennett blinked as the shock of Hazel's news ricocheted off him. Because he'd been sick enough to end up in the hospital, the navy had discharged a decent seaman? That seemed . . . harsh.

Seemed every time Bennett had talked to Hazel lately, something else had gone sideways. *Can she just catch a break already?* And Hunter? From Bennett's perspective, the guy's life had been a conveyor belt of one not-awesome event after another. *How will he ever know Your goodness?*

"Are you sure?" Bennett knew that was an inane response, but he couldn't help it.

Hazel shrugged into Bennett's dumbfounded reaction, but her face turned toward the ground as she nodded. "I guess. He said 'medically discharged' and that he's back to stay, because where else is he going to go?"

Wow. Bennett ran a hand through his hair, still processing this revelation. He thought about how this must have hit Hunter—which couldn't possibly be anything less than devastating. And Hazel? He'd been proud of her for making the trip to Nevada to see her brother, especially since she'd been so angry with him that she'd not spoken to him for over six months. Proud that she was coming around to a softness that was clearly never demonstrated to her.

Man, these Wallace siblings. Why would life just keep targeting these two?

"He's moved back into his room." Hazel lifted her eyes to look back at Hunter, a wariness in her look. "He should be back from town any minute. I can't imagine Janie is up for a *let's catch up* session with him . . ."

Bennett noted the trailing off of her voice. *Hunter and Janie . . .*

Huh. By Hazel's unspoken indication, there wasn't a chance in Luna—or even the actual moon—for that scenario. Then again, she'd just said that Hunter had gone to town specifically to see the woman who ran the local café. And he wouldn't be well received. Which was likely the case, as Bennett couldn't recall one good thing said about Hazel's brother from the likes of Janie.

That might be telling.

Shifting his fixation from that little intrigue, he refocused on what Hazel was trying to tell him. Hunter would be staying in the cabin. With them.

Maybe super awkward. Maybe the perfect excuse.

A cord of guilt tightened in his gut, and an involuntary replay of his last conversation with José intruded his conscience.

"You keeping it pure with her?" José prodded after Bennett told his new Christian friend about his girlfriend.

Bennett let his chin drop toward his chest as heat claimed his ears. Silence settled with weighty implication.

Then José nudged his shoulder. "You know what to do, man. Real love is honorable. And good men do hard things."

Old Bennett would have shot a sideways look at the man, told him to mind his own business and keep his personal standards to himself. And it all would have been a deflection, because even then—even when Bennett had deliberately lived as if there weren't a God of all creation who saw and knew all things—he'd felt the sharp sting of conscious as he'd lived the moral life of a garter snake.

But losing his memory had worked to remind him of who he had wanted to be, before he'd allowed anger and disillusionment to poison his life. Bennett wasn't that seared-soul man anymore. And he was working harder than ever to be that real, honorable man José had referenced. To become what his father had failed to be.

And that brought Bennett full circle, back to this moment with Hazel and the hard conversation he needed to have with her.

Hunter would be staying in the cabin. With them.

A fresh warning spiraled in Bennett's gut as this new reality sank again. But certainly not for the same reason that Hazel looked off kilter. And there he could place his focus. Not on the guilt José had multiplied or the awkwardness that Hunter's presence would certainly provoke.

Hazel.

Be what she needs in this moment.

His internal turmoil would have to wait. Bennett cupped her shoulders with both hands. "This is a big deal. Are you okay?"

Hazel shrugged. Worry creased her brow and sufficed as her answer through the mossy-green color of her eyes.

Poor Hazel. The woman liked dependability and hated the unexpected. The highest value, in her estimation, was fierce independence—which was both admirable and utterly infuriating. Her life had been brimming with the unexpected lately, and more than once she'd been thrust into a position of vulnerability. Adjusting course was not really in Hazel's skill set. Nor was trusting another human being.

Both triggered conflict in their relationship. Even so . . . He stared down at this tough little mite of a woman. Where he'd once seen a badger lady, now he saw a hidden fragility that he still didn't understand.

But he wanted with all of his heart to protect her.

Bennett rubbed Hazel's arms. "How about Hunter? Is he okay?"

Those green eyes pinched. "I don't understand why he came back."

"This is his home."

While her chin dropped, Hazel shook her head. "This was never home to Hunter. He said so himself. That was why he wanted you to buy—"

Sighing, Bennett pulled her against his chest and wrapped her up close before she could finish that story. Last thing he wanted was to have her upset with him all over again over the way they'd met. When she wound her arms around him and pressed her head into his button-down shirt, relief unknotted his shoulders.

At least they were past that.

Bennett couldn't imagine that Hunter was okay. For all he knew, Hunter intended to be a career military man. That was the life he'd chosen, and he hadn't given any indication that he'd changed his mind. And even if not that, Bennett was certain that Hazel was right—Hunter had never intended to come back to live at Elk Canyon. The very reason Bennett had ever set foot in Luna, or this cabin, in the first place had been to ensure Hunter was done with this place forever.

What had propelled the man to come back? It had to be more than the navy's dismissal. Certainly Hunter would have had options. John Brighton sprang to mind, and Bennett felt certain Hunter's commanding officer would have helped him find a new career path if Hunter had wanted it.

But he'd chosen to come home.

Could Hunter be looking for restoration? Hope for that very thing filled Bennett's chest so quickly and completely that it almost hurt. What would it mean to have Hunter and Hazel reconcile?

It might mean a whole lot of good for both Hazel and Hunter—for all of them, really. But it seemed like almost too lofty a hope to really grab on to . . .

Almost. Then again, Bennett knew a Guy.

Thirteen

"It's quite a spectacular view."

The sound of Bennett's voice startled Hunter out of his semiconscious existence. He jerked forward, away from the tree trunk he'd been lounging against, and spun on the rock beneath his backside to see his sister's boyfriend moseying down the trail toward him.

"I didn't know you knew that trail."

"I noted where you disappeared to earlier. Wasn't too hard to follow."

Grabbing a fresh bottle of mountain stream–chilled brew, Hunter pried off the top and took a long swig. "Look at you, becoming a mountain man. Who is more shocked, you or Hazel?"

Though Hunter hadn't invited him to, and had failed to offer a beer when he'd gotten his own, Bennett lowered himself onto a nearby boulder and stretched as if settling in.

Huh. Well then, maybe they'd just have a chat.

"For the record, I know you're sleeping with my sister." Hunter slid a side glance, one brow lifted, toward Bennett.

The man met his gaze for a moment, then looked toward the small lake below their perch, his shoulders rounding. After a pause in which crimson snuck up his neck, Bennett rubbed that heated skin and then nodded.

A strange response. Hunter had known Bennett in college and remembered his reputation with the girls. It'd been along the lines of *take what you can get and never regret it*. Come to think of it, what had Hunter been thinking, sending Bennett up to Elk Canyon with only his little sister on the premises? That had been incredibly stupid.

Or maybe it'd just been destiny?

Whatever. It hardly mattered now and wasn't what this weird conversation was about anyway. Hunter had opened with that stark proclamation only because Bennett had insisted on bunking with him the night before. That had made everything weird. Weird*er*, and had also had made Hazel grumpier. So Hunter had just out-with-it said what was true. It was supposed to help, not jack up the tension more.

Well. Maybe that wasn't true. He'd spat that out of his mouth from pure irritation—mostly left over from his two-day-old conversation with Janie. But some because of the unbearable awkwardness of the night before. Talk about third-wheeling. It didn't get worse than that.

This shouldn't be that big of deal. Two guys talking, was all.

Perhaps because they were talking about his sister? Hunter shook his head. They all just needed to find a way to make things work, because Hunter needed sleep.

"Aside from the weirdness of this conversation, I don't care," Hunter said. "Just thought you should know I know. You don't have to bunk with me. That's all I'm saying."

Bennett glanced at him again but still looked uncomfortable.

"Look. You're both grown adults. It's not really my business." And yet there they were talking about it. And, frankly, it sort of made Hunter mad, come to think of it. He'd sent Bennett up to Elk Canyon for one reason and one reason only—buy the mountain. Instead he'd taken up with Hunter's sister while simultaneously ruining Hunter's perfect plan for finally getting himself and Hazel out of Luna. "Although I think it's bizarre that you're dating a woman who tricked you into believing you were married, I'm fine with you being with Hazel. As long as you don't treat her like one of your college conquests . . ."

"She's not that. Definitely not that—and I'm not that guy anymore." Bennet's response sounded about as relaxed as a man jumping out of a plane. Without a parachute. "I'm glad you don't have a problem with us dating." He cleared his throat, straightened his posture, and squeezed his fingers against his legs. Another long break extended in the peculiar conversation. Then Bennett rolled his shoulders again and turned to look at Hunter. "I love her. I want to marry her."

Marry? Hazel?

Though it was rude, especially since Bennett was sincere and this was a weighty discussion, Hunter snorted as he lifted the chilled amber bottle in his right hand. "Good luck with that."

Bennett's ironed posture collapsed again, and he stared over the lake as he adjusted his hat. "Yeah."

Suddenly Hunter leaned forward. "You asked her?"

"Not like proposed, asked." Bennett's jaw worked stiffly. "But it's come up."

"By the sound of that, it didn't go like you hoped." And no one who knew Hazel would be one bit surprised . . .

With a slow headshake, Bennett turned his defeated expression back to Hunter. "She says she never thought she'd get married. I thought maybe that's because she believed she'd never meet someone who would want to do life with her. But—"

Bennett didn't finish, and he didn't need to. Hunter knew.

Hunter pointed to the small stream of water flowing to his left, where he'd sank a six-pack—now minus one—of bottles into the snowmelt. "Sounds like you'd better grab one of those. Can't beat the chill of a mountain stream."

Bennett slunk off the rock he'd been sitting on, snagged a bottle, and popped the top. He took a slow drink, lowered back onto the bolder, and set the bottle down.

Water rippled, birds flitted through the air, and a chilly breeze swished through the evergreen boughs. And Bennett had nothing more to say.

Finally, Hunter spoke again. "Marriage didn't always look like a daydream in our world."

"I get that. My parents are divorced, so I do get that." Bennett squinted, the direction of his look pointed toward the cabin hidden by the rise separating the larger lake from this smaller one. Then he turned his study to Hunter. "But did *you* decide that marriage was a bad deal?"

Hunter swallowed. How did the uncomfortable end of this talk get turned on him? With a shrug, he tried to play it off as *no big deal*. "No. But I'm a guy. Things might look different from my view."

Bennett's study morphed from quizzical to suspicious. Then he nodded. "Janie."

"What?" Talk about coming from left field . . .

"She stole the phone straight out of my hand that very first day when she found out you were on the other end of that call. She was madder than the raccoon that was trapped in the bunkhouse with me later that night."

"So?" Was the heat crawling up Hunter's neck as red as it had been on Bennett at the start of this conversation?

"That kind of reaction must have a backstory." Bennett's brows rose farther. "Hazel said you went to Luna your first morning back. To see Janie."

"Why would she think that?" Man. That sun was getting hot. "I didn't say so."

"Good question. Another good question is why would she think Janie wouldn't want to catch up with you?" He air quoted "catch up."

It was Hunter's turn to fasten a hard stare on the lake.

"I see," Bennett said. "How long did you date her?"

"Three years."

"You must have been kids."

"Basically."

"But you loved her?"

Hunter pressed his lips tight and continued to stare at the blue-green water below.

"Were you engaged?"

Finally Hunter turned his head to pin an annoyed look onto Bennett. "History you don't need to know."

"I'll take that as a yes. Who called it off?"

Hunter spat the sour taste from his mouth. "She did."

Their gazes held. An understanding gentled Bennett's expression, and he nodded. "It's been a long time for you to keep away."

"She wasn't the reason I stayed away. I never wanted to live here. Hazel doesn't want to get married, and I didn't want to live here, and we both have our reasons."

"And you'll both cling to them like they'll somehow save you from the past you hate." Bennett shook his head as his brow creased. "Even if your reasons are the very thing sucking the joy and life from your soul."

The pulse in Hunter's head throbbed painfully. He wanted to cover his ears. He wanted to grip Bennett by his shirtfront and shake him. He wanted to plow his fist into something.

His military discipline wouldn't acquiesce to his knee-jerk temper. Instead he rolled his fists and squeezed his eyes shut.

A hand covered his shoulder, causing him to lurch away. Bennett stood, holding his hands up. "I'm sorry. That was maybe too far."

Yeah. It was. What did Bennett know about how Hunter's life had been there at Elk Canyon? Nothing. He could guarantee Bennett knew *nothing*, because not even Hazel knew the whole of it.

But . . .

There was some truth to what Bennett had said and the way things had worked out, Hunter was going to have to face it. He was tired of having, as Bennett put it, the joy and life sucked out of his soul.

He was tired of running, and he had run out of places to go.

"You came back."

Hunter shook his head, still staring at the rippling gray waters. "It was like I *had* to. The cosmos demanded it."

It seemed so stupid, and yet that was the only way Hunter knew how to put it. He hadn't *wanted* to come back. But he couldn't fight the mandate for it.

"What will you do now?" Bennett's question fell quietly in the extended silence between them.

Hunter shrugged. "This is a good view." Gesturing toward the smaller lake with his bottle, he returned to the opening of their conversation.

Bennett crossed his arms, and his gaze traveled the panorama of the vista. "Every bit as good as the one from the cabin." He dared to step forward and clapped Hunter's shoulder. "Maybe you were sent back for a purpose."

"What would you imagine that would be?"

"Might be *God* sent you. Maybe He has some redemption on these shores for you, Hunt."

"You believe that?" Hunter spoke the words with sarcasm. "God would send me here for redemption?" Even with the heavy weight of doubt in his mind, he couldn't deny the surge of hope flooding his chest.

Bennett made eye contact. "I do." He held that look for one beat longer and then started back down the trail. "But what I think doesn't matter a whole lot."

Hunter watched the man as he retreated back toward the cabin. Toward Hazel and the life they'd mysteriously found on the shores of the larger lake just over the ridge.

Was their relationship Hazel's redemption? Or was it Bennett's? Was it even redemption at all or just some bizarre quirk of fate?

It's redemption . . . at least a little.

Hunter didn't bother to wonder where that thought emerged from. He was too fixated on the question that immediately followed.

Could there be redemption for him there too?

Fourteen

Slouched against the back window as he sprawled out in the bed of his pickup, Hunter scrolled through the local market listings on Facebook. All six of them.

Man, Luna was small town. Not what he'd wanted for the rest of his life. Even if the girl he *had* wanted for the rest of his life was rooted there.

At that, his mind drifted back to the morning two days past. Against all rational actions, Hunter had taken his truck back down that rough mountain road on the north ridge just to see her pretty face.

Had he imagined that she'd meet him with anything better than a frown? Yeah, actually. He had. After all, he'd nearly died. At least had landed in the hospital for a week and had been sick enough to be discharged from the navy.

A bitter taste smeared on his tongue. He tried to drown it with a slug of stream-chilled Blue Moon. Given his heritage, that wasn't smart. But smart didn't figure into this solo homecoming party.

He'd thought maybe his brush with death would have stirred up something other than resentment in Janie's heart. After all, she had nearly married him.

Nope. Not the case. Janie hadn't cared one bit. Might be that she maybe even hoped he'd exit her life forever by way of the hospital basement.

Pain sliced through his chest. How could he still care about a woman who clearly despised him so utterly?

Pathetic.

Hunter tipped back another swig and then returned to the screen in his palm. Swiping up, he stopped on the single post that had caught his mild interest.

It was old. But still functional. Small. But he'd done small before.

He looked at the price again. Well within his separation pay.

Lifting his eyes, Hunter let his gaze travel over the view Bennett had called spectacular. It was. And out of Hazel's visual range, which would help all of them. And it was a spot that held few of his memories—another favorable check mark.

He lifted the phone and imagined the trailer set up there. It was an eyesore. But it wouldn't be permanent. Just a beginning. A place to crash while he figured out the rest of the plan budding in his mind.

Hazel would hate it. The trailer, and more, the plan. Not just a little. She would absolutely *despise* the whole of it.

But he needed a life. A hope and a future. And this was his land too. One way or another, he was going to claim what should be his as well as hers.

He would do it.

Tomorrow he'd go buy that tin can on wheels. And then . . .

And then he'd figure out the rest. Hazel was just going to have to put on her big-girl pants and get over it.

Janie wiped down the butcher-block counter, careful to look for brown rings left behind by coffee mugs after multiple refills. That Old Man Coffee Club. They could sure put down the steaming cups of caffeine while they solved all Luna's problems.

Good thing they didn't know about the things that turned around her mind at night, keeping her awake. She could imagine the stream of advice she'd get from that bunch.

Business tight right now? What you need is a man to manage the big stuff.

Yeah. Because men did super well managing big stuff. In her limited experience, men cowered at the big stuff and preferred to chase down easy living.

More likely what you need is to settle down. Get married, girl. Raise some kids and let this little shop go.

That one, likely from Marely, would pierce like a fiery dart, for more than one reason. Her café wasn't a piddly little shop. It was her vision and freaking hard work, for heaven's sake. And the other reason . . .

She wasn't going to ponder the other reason. Not when Hunter could stroll in at any time since he had decided Luna was his only option left. Sheesh, what was that anyway? There was a big old country out there. Fifty whole states and other nations as backup. And Hunter had tucked his tail and wandered back to itsy-bitsy Luna? The one spot on the planet he said he couldn't live?

What gives?

Stalking back to her kitchen, Janie slapped the dirty rag on the rim of the stainless-steel sink the same moment the bell at the front door chimed.

Deep breath. Pleasant expression. Nothing bothering her . . . She was sunshine and sparkles. Warm summer breezes and morning birdsongs . . .

Janie walked back through the swinging door and stopped short of reaching the counter. Her shoulders sagged, and the tension twisting her gut released.

"Hazel." A genuine grin eased the beginnings of a tension headache at her temple. "Twice in less than ten days? What brings you down again?"

"My stupid brother."

Ah. The thing they loathed together. The tension regained its hold. Janie raised her brows. "What's he done now?"

"You haven't heard?"

"You already told me he's home for good. Or . . . you know, whatever." Janie shook her head as the line *for worse* trailed through her thoughts. "And he showed up here to confirm that."

A single brow arched over Hazel's bright-green eyes. "Yes, he said. How did that go?"

Janie crossed her arms. "He came. He went. Whatever." Even if Hazel was her best friend and they had spent half their lives practically as sisters, Janie wasn't going to dive into the whole black pit of *how that went*.

Mostly because Janie didn't want to say out loud how ugly she'd been

Hazel stepped closer. "You okay?"

"Of course."

As she saddled up a stool, Hazel studied Janie as if she didn't believe her claim for a single breath.

Janie waved off the silent concern and summoned a conspirator's grin. "The bigger question is, how is it going up at the cabin between you two?"

All concern crashed into a fierce scowl. "That's the thing."

"You look like you're ready to fight a bear."

"That would be an easier win."

"Uh-oh. Don't kill him, okay?" Janie bent and leaned toward her friend with her elbows pressed against the counter. "Jail wasn't so fun, remember?"

"Don't bring that up in the middle of my fury. Hunter won't stand a chance."

Janie snorted a laugh. "Maybe you should suggest he move out to the shack or something."

Those green eyes darkened to something murky, hot, and terrifying. "That's the problem."

"What?"

"He is moving out."

Hunter was running scared again? That didn't take long. Janie vehemently denied that the sinking in her chest was disappointment. What was there to be disappointed about? She wanted him to leave.

Right.

More like she'd known he would leave. Again. And she was right, and that was infuriating.

"Where is he going now?" That came off as passive. Surely it did.

"Nowhere." Hazel slapped the counter. "He *bought* himself that trash can of a camper trailer from Jasper. And he's roped *my boyfriend* into helping him get it all level and set over at the south cove."

"The south cove?" Janie was processing *all* of what Hazel had just spat out. Trash can camper trailer? From Jasper Lingle? She didn't know he had a trailer of any variety.

As far as Janie knew, the archaic man only left his house long enough to grab a cup of coffee from her café and a newspaper from the stand outside of Mama's store. Then it was back to his house—if it was the summer, sitting on the front porch of that once-upon-a-time-it-was-yellow house, or if it was winter, staring out of the filmy, dirt-streaked window that faced Main Street.

A fellow like that surely wouldn't own a camper trailer. Why would he? Then again, why would Hunter buy it?

"The little lake that connects to mine by the narrow falls?" Hazel's fiery anger was *not* cooling.

It took a second for Janie to regain what they were talking about from her side trip about Jasper Lingle's personal habits. The little lake . . . ah, yes. The south cove. Janie knew the place well. And she was right back with Hazel.

Huh.

Her lake. That was what Hazel had called it. Not theirs—hers *and* her brother's, by legal right granted in the grandmother's will. Which was, in fact, the actual fact. This might be one of the reasons Hazel and Hunter were always locking horns. Janie loved her, but Hazel might need a dose of reality and some corrective measures for her myopic vision. Especially when it came to anything that had to do with the cabin and Elk Canyon. And her brother.

Janie, however, would not be the one to give that smack of reality to her best friend. Not when she was all bear-fighting mad and everything. And also, not about Hunter.

She didn't want anything to do with Hunter.

". . . he's just going to set up camp for who knows how long and ruin the place. I don't want a KOA starting up on my land!"

"Whoa!" Janie grabbed Hazel's arm. She'd missed who knew how much of whatever Hazel had just said, but she was pretty sure Hazel would hyperventilate in this overdrawn hysteria she had going on. "Who said anything about a KOA?" That was a campground thing, right?

Janie might should have gotten out of Luna a little more than she had. If she were a braver person, maybe she would have . . .

Hazel crossed her arms as her brows gathered together like a little forehead storm cloud. "It was an expression."

"No it isn't. Never heard KOA used as an expression." Janie raised her brows and mirrored Hazel's crossed arms. "It was an exaggeration."

Hazel shot her the squinty eyes.

Squinty eyes were what teachers gave misbehaving students. Or Mama issued for certain corrective measures—which, let it be known, never failed for Janie's mom. Even old Jasper complied with the squinty eyes.

You take that can of green beans, Jasper Lingle, and you eat them. Don't you dare toss them out. No neighbor of mine is going to die of scurvy because he won't eat his fruits and vegetables.

Hazel had the squinty eyes down pretty well. Had since she'd been thirteen. But they weren't thirteen anymore, and for the record Janie was the older of the pair anyway.

Propping her hands on her hips, Janie shifted her stance, as if she might need a steadier base. "Look. This might be the best deal for both of you. Hunter's got a place to land while he licks his poor wounded pride, and you've still got the cabin to yourself. Win-win. No need to get dramatic."

"I am *never* dramatic."

With a snort, Janie shook her head. "You're not a lot of girly-type things, Zel, that's for darn sure. But drama is definitely in your arsenal."

"What?" She looked crestfallen, the way a cheerleader might look if someone said there was no cheerleading allowed. Which was an amusing comparison that Janie tried not to bring up and laugh out loud about.

"Don't worry." She managed to suppress a grin. "You're still you. Tough, independent, a little odd. Just with drama mixed in. And I'll always love you."

Hazel stood there deflated.

Better than erupting with volcanic levels of fury. Which was also a common Hazel response. But Janie wasn't saying that out loud either.

"Anyway, back to the issue. I'm sure Hunter won't stay in a tin can of a camper for long."

"Trash can."

"Okay, trash can. Which makes it more certain. Hunter always wanted more out of life than Luna. He's not going to settle permanently in a *trash can*. Specifically, one presumably incapable of traveling past the town limits."

One suspicious brow arched over Hazel's muddied green eyes. "He's up to something."

"What could that be?"

"I don't know. But..." Hazel tipped her head to the side, and her expression took on the *I've got a plan* quality that Janie knew too well.

Well enough to know she wasn't going to like whatever Zel said next.

"...you can find out."

Yep. Definitely did *not* like it.

"Nope." Janie held both hands up. "No way. Not going to do that. Talk to your boyfriend. Better yet, just duke it out with your brother like an adult. I'm out."

"I'm currently *not* talking to my boyfriend. Or my brother."

"That sounds grown up."

Hazel hit her with the squinty eyes again. "How long did you and Hunter go without speaking?"

"Not even close to the same." Janie let her shoulders sag as she turned away. Hazel didn't mean to pick at a seeping wound. As far as she knew, that deep cut had long since healed. Cauterized by his swift exit from Janie's life.

And it should have. That was exactly what should have been true.

"Look." Hazel tried a new tone. The one that usually gave her the win. "He came to town, to this café, to see you basically first thing. What you think still matters to him."

Another knife twist. Janie sucked in a silent, sharp breath.

"And he'll tell you the truth. He always has."

Not always. Pain throbbed in her chest.

"Can't you just ask him yourself?" It took way too much effort for Janie to speak without allowing her voice to wobble.

"Like he tells me anything."

A bad family habit. Janie shut her eyes. She already knew she'd be doing it. Though she'd said no way right off, she'd known deep down that . . .

"Please, Janie?"

. . . she'd do it for her best friend. Else that was what she'd tell herself, because that made her far less pathetic than admitting other things.

A sigh emptied from the deepest depths of her lungs as she turned back to face Hazel. "You owe me."

Those green eyes softened toward mossy amber. "All my undying love."

"You've already sworn to that. And already it's a lie." Janie cleared her throat. "Might I submit Bennett Crofton as proof. I do not have *all* your undying love."

"Leave him out of this. Anyway, I'm a simple mountain girl. What else could I possibly give?"

"Whatever I ask for in the future. If I survive."

"You're not scared of Hunter."

Not true. The thought of seeing him made her heart race and blood burn. But there was the slight possibility that wasn't fear at all. Or, perhaps more likely, that it was fear, just not of Hunter.

Not directly.

Janie turned toward the kitchen, waving as she made her escape before the heat could tint her cheeks. "You owe me. Write it down, and count on me calling it in."

Fifteen

Bennett's silence was telling.

Not what Hunter had hoped for after laying out his new life plans to his old friend and new sort-of brother-in-lawish guy.

Hunter leaned his full weight against the back of the canvas folding lawn chair—a risky move, as he didn't know how long the pair he'd found inside the fifteen-foot camper had left. If the faded teal color and the frayed hems along the arms were any indication, he was leaning against the final threads. Literally.

But he pressed his back against the straining fabric anyway as he returned Bennett's study.

"You're an investment genius, Crofton, which was why I called you a year ago. And I know this is a solid plan." He leaned against the arm of the chair, which groaned under the strain of his weight. "Look me in the eye and tell me I'm wrong."

With a turn of his chin, Bennett looked him in the eye. "You're not wrong. As a financial scheme at least. It's a beautiful spot, an amazing view. And those high-end hunting lodges can be lucrative. You're not wrong on any of that—even if the initial investment will be steep. A road that won't scare that kind of clientele away, a building that will attract the kind of customers who will be lifetime returners, high-end furnishings. And employees—because there's no way you're going to manage it all on your own. Starting with the food . . ." He held up the fire-roasted hot dog, wrapped in Wonder bread, that Hunter had given him to eat and arched a critical eyebrow.

"I know. I have thought of all of that. I've been working on a written plan . . ." Hunter used the arms of that end-of-its-life chair to push up to his feet.

Bennett held a hand up, stopping him before he straightened. "I'm not saying yes."

"But you haven't even—"

"Hazel will never agree to this, Hunter. You know she will throw a holy fit."

Hunter slumped back into his chair and pinned a heated glare on Bennett. "Hazel throws a holy fit on a regular basis. Honestly, man, I don't know how you put up with her."

"Easy, now. She is your sister." Bennett's frown matched the warning tone of his voice. "And the woman I love. Let's not get into the ring about it."

"That's weird."

"What's weird?"

"You really love her." The statement came out more wonder than questioning.

"Don't you want your sister to have a life? Isn't that why you were undermining her by sending me up here in the first place? You said she needed more than—"

"Yes." Hunter swallowed and moved his attention toward the lake view. It really was something from right there. The spot he'd picked was a perched vista framed by a ridge to the north, shielding the view of the big lake, their cabin, and the spruce-covered hill to the south that rolled gently downward until it met the sparkling waters of the smaller lake below.

To his left—toward the cabin—a veillike waterfall sprayed twelve feet from the ridge into the inlet of his lake. The sound of water splashing married with the whisper of the breeze through the trees and the sporadic chirping of mountain bluebirds. Hunter pictured the wide covered front deck of his lodge facing those falls and the smaller lake. An unmatched panoramic view. In his vision he'd place a line of heavy log-hewn rockers ready to accommodate a guest after a day of guided hunting.

It would be idyllic. And profitable. He was certain of it.

But they'd left the topic of his plans and had shifted to his sister's life. That always seemed the way of things in Hunter's world. Hazel was the priority. Mostly, he wanted it that way. She did matter a whole lot to him—and he'd taken some dark blows for her to prove it. Blows she still knew nothing about.

But.

"What about me, Bennett?" Hunter turned back to the other man. "I'm not meaning to come off as a selfish jerk here—even if that's what you think of me. Hazel matters to me. More than it might look like, more than she understands. I hate that there is constant animosity between her and me. Honest. I never wanted it and didn't plan it that way. But there are simply things in our past that aren't reconcilable. I tried to leave. I tried to let her have this on her own and build a new life. Obviously that didn't work out, and I didn't have a choice. So where does that leave me? This land, it's mine too, you know? Shouldn't I get a chance to make something good out of a life that wasn't great? To claim this inheritance that was left for me and try to make a life from it?" Frustration, passion, desperation . . . they all filled his voice as the words tumbled from his lips.

For a moment, the exposure made him shake.

"You were the one who brought up redemption. You said you believed—" Throat swelling, Hunter cut off and didn't finish.

Because he wanted it. The redemption. Even if he still couldn't believe it was possible.

With eyes pinched and a brow furrowed, Bennett listened, and when Hunter came to the end, Bennett's study shifted away from Hunter and toward the lake. Several beats went by in silence, causing Hunter to shutter himself away behind anger that came readily.

But then Bennett nodded. Slowly. "I get it." He looked at Hunter, the sincerity in his expression a line of hope. "I get it, Hunt. And yes, I think it's fair that you get a shot at a life here too." His brow folded with deeper lines as he rubbed the rough shadow of his jaw. "It's just . . . complicated."

"Things with the Wallaces have always been complicated." A loaded statement. Bennett didn't know the half of it, and Hunter doubted he ever would.

Again, Bennett nodded.

The chair creaked as Hunter leaned forward, pressing his elbows against his legs. "You have a way with Hazel."

"I'm not sure I want between you two."

"You already are. And maybe that's providential."

"All of the sudden you believe in providence?"

Hunter shrugged. "I don't know what I believe. Brighton . . ." Never mind John Brighton right now. That might be a conversation for another time. Maybe. He cleared his throat. "I'm pretty sure that *you* believe in providence. Or else you wouldn't have given Hazel a second thought when she was locked up for what she did to you."

Bennett chuckled and then sent Hunter a sober glance. "I believe God is willing to go to extreme lengths to get our attention, if that is what you mean. But for the record, I'm not sure I would have said that back then."

"You were pretty mad."

"Yes I was."

"Then?"

"I saw my role in it. And then I saw who I'd become in life—the broader view. I didn't like it, and it suddenly occurred to me that I wouldn't have seen that I needed to change if it hadn't been for that week up here with her. I was a different man that week—a whole lot more like the man I *wanted* to be."

That was a strange, twisted path that Hunter still wasn't sure he could comprehend. Maybe he never would. However, there was the matter of his sister's happiness—and he could see plain as the shimmering water in front of him that Bennett made Hazel happy. And generally, a better person. He could also acknowledge that Bennett seemed steadier, more grounded in who he was.

Wasn't sure that was Hazel's doing though. Might have a whole lot more to do with what Bennett had just said—that God went to extreme measures to get his attention. Which brought back John Brighton's claim full circle.

God has good intentions for you, Wallace. His ways don't make sense sometimes, but He does have a plan for you, to give you a hope and a future.

Didn't make sense to Hunter—God allowing him to get sick, to have his lungs damaged to the point of uselessness, to lose his place in the navy . . . But Bennett's story didn't make a whole lot of sense either. Yet there they were.

Hunter sighed. "Will you help me with this? Even if you don't want to invest—no hard feeling there, I swear. I have other options. But Hazel . . ."

Standing, Bennett stretched his back, drew a deep breath, and looked toward the falls. Likely, he wasn't seeing the water but the woman who lived in the cabin beyond.

It was a tough ask, and Hunter knew it. Hazel had inherited their grandfather's immovable personality. Stubborn to a fault. And generally unaware of how her iron resolve might crush others.

"I'll try."

Hunter's head snapped up. His attention flew from his shoes to Bennett. "Yeah?"

Bennett nodded, though doubt clouded his expression. "I can't promise you anything. You know Hazel . . ."

"Yeah, I do. But you'll talk to her?"

"I will. You'll give it some time for her to come to terms with it before you move forward?"

"You mean you think I should?"

"Send me what you have on paper. But just sitting right here? I can see. It could work. It could be . . . amazing."

"So you're in?" Man, Hunter had hoped for this. But hadn't dared to believe that maybe . . .

"No promises on that. I've got some other irons going, and Hazel—" Bennett rubbed his neck and then dropped his hand, letting it smack against his thigh. "Even if I don't put money into this, I think you should go for it." Stepping forward, Bennett clapped Hunter's shoulder twice. "It's your land too. Your life. Just, promise me that you'll try. With Hazel, I mean. She wouldn't be so mad at you if you didn't matter to her, you know?"

A swirl of adrenaline tangled Hunter's thoughts as he stood. Elation. Fear. And the frustration that seemed to be his constant companion, because there was always something weighing him down, holding him back.

He focused on the excitement and left the other two pending to deal with later.

"Hunter."

Bennett's demand jolted him back to the moment.

"Your sister. You have to promise—"

Hunter nodded. "I'll try. I'll keep trying."

The excitement dimmed as that frustration took spotlight again. He would do exactly that—keep trying with Hazel.

But the truth was, he didn't think it'd matter much. She would never bend, and they would always be broken.

Sixteen

Janie followed the smell of grilling meat as she left her nineties Jeep Cherokee parked at a slight angle where the road had faded to little more than a pair of freshly pressed tire tracks. It had been a long time since she'd been on this side of the south ridge. And she puzzled over what exactly she was doing there now.

The falls . . . A sad, achy twist rolled in her gut. The falls had been sacred ground to them. So of course he would choose that spot to land. And of course Hazel would send Janie there to him.

She was so pliable. Such a sucker.

Keeping her feet on the tire tracks, Janie stepped her way toward the slender plume of gray smoke—Hunter's campsite. The late afternoon felt cool as she treaded under the cover of tall pines and stately spruce. Absently, she noted that the yellow bells and bitterroot were still blooming at this altitude—a full two weeks since Luna had seen the last of the yellows and pinks of those wildflowers. Their cheerful colors caused a wisp of a grin to lift her lips, replacing what had certainly been a scowl. At least there was beauty up here for her to feast her soul upon before she faced, yet again, the one she didn't want to see.

The path cut downward for twelve feet and then leveled off. Ahead of her, a vista opened to the minor lake. Wow. She'd forgotten the full splendor.

Hunter sure did know how to pick a good spot. Always had.

To her left, a meadow sprawled out all lush green and dotted with the pinks and yellows, with the addition of magenta buds swaying in the breeze. Fireweed. It would soon burst open, replacing the bitterroot and yellow bells as the star of the wildflower show. Blue columbine would join with its clear sky color, as well as the true red of the Indian Paint brush. With the water in the middle ground, and the rolling hills that separated Elk Canyon from Luna in the backdrop, the scene would be nothing less than stunning.

Except for that awful camper Janie caught a glimpse of in the corner of her vision.

Trash-can trailer. For once, Hazel had not been exaggerating. What was supposed to be white on that metal heap of garbage was freckled heavily with rust splotches. The green stripe in the middle appeared closer to the color of manure.

Yeah. Hunter sure knew how to pick 'em.

Janie shook her head just as the door to that aluminum disaster flew open, smacking against the side of the camper with a crack. The man himself came forth, ducking out the narrow doorway with an empty plate in one hand and a long metal spatula in the other. Unaware he was not alone, Hunter whistled their old high school fight song as he moseyed to his Solo Stove, waving his spatula in the air as if conducting the high school band.

She couldn't help it. Janie snorted.

Hunter stopped dead, his back jamming ramrod straight, his flailing hand pausing in the air midmotion.

Smug satisfaction curled up in Janie's chest and settled in for a comfortable nap. She crossed her arms and tilted her head as he slowly turned to face her.

"I see you finally made drum major."

His brows pinched as his hand lowered. "What are you doing here?"

"Came to see if Hazel was telling tales." Janie motioned to the camper. "I see she wasn't inflating your sad state of affairs."

"What?"

"Trash-can trailer. That's what she called it."

Hunter looked at his newly acquired living quarters. "A man's home is his castle. Don't be dogging mine."

"One strong gust off the peaks will roll you straight into the lake."

"Wouldn't you just love that?"

Janie raised her brows as if she just might.

He lowered the spatula until it rested against his jeans. "I'll ask you again, what are you doing here?"

"Already said."

"Not buying that. You made it as clear as the mountain water that you didn't want to see me the last time I was in town. Even the persuasion of my angry sister isn't likely to change your ridiculously stubborn mind."

"Shows how well you really know me. I'm here exactly on behalf of your sister—and yeah, she's madder than a mama bear."

"When isn't she?" He turned back toward his smoldering fire pit, on top of which two meat patties sizzled. With a wave of his spatula, he invited her into his *living room*. "I suppose I'm obligated to offer you some of my supper."

"Don't strain yourself trying to be a gentleman."

With a backward glance, he shot her a hard, unimpressed look. "I won't. Not with you. Wouldn't matter anyway."

His dry tone sliced deep. At one time he'd done all the gentleman things to impress her. Held doors. Hung up her coat. Fetched seconds. Whispered pretty words . . . Whatever he could think of.

He'd meant every gesture. Every word.

"Cut the crap, Hunter." She stomped toward the fire and planted herself on the opposite side of the rolling smoke. Crossing her arms again, she pinned him with a glare. "What are you doing here with that piece of junk?"

"Living."

"You can't be serious."

"Why not? It's my property too. And that cabin is way too small. Three's a crowd and all."

"Bennett doesn't live there."

"He's there now."

"For the weekend."

"He says he's in love with her." Hunter feigned an exaggerated shudder. "Which is bizarre." He shook his head. "Anyway, his stays are bound to get longer than weekend-long visits, and I'm not here for *that*."

At his puke expression, Janie let her arms fall as a chuckle escaped. "They are an unmatched pair, aren't they?"

From the shoulders down, Hunter visibly relaxed and even let a grin slip onto his mouth. Goodness, but the man was handsome. More so than he'd been at twenty, and back then she hadn't been able to imagine a better-looking guy. Sucking in a breath, Janie looked toward the rocky path at her feet. "They're happy together," she said weakly.

"Yeah." Hunter's soft whisper held undercurrents that Janie thought she understood. The kind that swept through the wreckage of broken dreams and splintered hopes and tugged against the skeletal remains that had once been all beauty and life. "I'm glad."

And yet, beyond reason, there remained something anchored and subtly lovely. A lasting, quiet hope . . . These currents were complicated. And compelling.

She looked up to find sincerity in his expression backing up the claim. It shouldn't surprise her. Hunter had cared deeply about his little sister. He'd made a whole lot of sacrifices for her, and even bore some physical scars from his efforts to protecting her.

This.

This was why Janie had fallen for her best friend's brother. Though he'd been but a youth back then, he'd shouldered the weight of manly responsibilities, and he had been good.

He's still a good man . . .

The soft thread weaving in her heart, through her mind, was unnerving. She had no idea if it was the truth. They'd not seen each other in years, except in a few scattered moments—anger, tension-filled moments—when he'd come home to check on Hazel. Their contact had been limited to bitter exchanges pursued only when absolutely necessary.

Hunter could be a waste of possibilities. He could be an arrogant user of women. A hopeless closet alcoholic—he had that in his genes. He could be a demanding jerk.

As she stood there in the peace of the forest, etched in a scene that had once been like a fairy tale to her young and wildly-in-love heart, looking at the man who had played the leading role to hers in that long-past love-swept moment, she couldn't believe any of those possibilities be true.

He could still be the man she'd loved.

She had a yearning to believe the whisper.

He is still a good man . . .

"Have supper with me?" Hunter's gentle invitation stirred that longing deeper.

A battle commenced within. The surge of war knocked her emotions unsteady as one side demanded she hold her ground, keep her resentment, and hold him responsible for the bitter disappointment he'd lodged there. The other urged humility. Understanding. And forgiveness.

Which would win?

Hunter turned back to his Solo Stove and flipped the pair of hamburger patties.

"Looks like only enough for one," Janie said.

He shrugged. "I've survived with less."

She patted her belly. "I'm actually not hungry." True story. Her stomach roiled full with turmoil.

Hunter snorted. "You just don't trust my cooking."

"Could be that. You were never very good at it."

"I can burn meat with the best of them." He gestured to a cut log, turned on one end like a stool. Likely he had intended to use it as a table, while he sat on the other of the matched pair.

Janie met him halfway by sitting but still refused the meat patty sandwiched between Wonder bread.

"Did you forget to buy buns?"

"Mama Bulldog didn't have any. Said a large family bought her out early this week on their way through town and wouldn't be getting more until Monday's truck comes."

"Ah." Janie nodded.

"Maybe you should bake fresh buns, hmm?" Hunter bit into his supper. No ketchup. No mustard. No anything to mask the burnt patty he'd charbroiled.

Ew.

Janie looked away so she wouldn't choke on his behalf. "I don't have time for that."

"Business is good?"

"It is. For a town like Luna. And it's just me, so . . ." She folded her hands and settled them on her knees. With raised brows, she met his gaze. "Surprised?"

"That you're doing well?" Those intense eyes held on her for a moment, causing her heart to ooze with heat. "Not one bit."

Oh man. How was it possible to feel both pleasure and guilt at the same time?

Janie swallowed and looked at the fingers she'd laced together as he dismantled another one of her false accusations. The one that seethed that Hunter didn't believe in her. Didn't think that she'd make it as a businesswoman on her own. That he'd wanted to whisk her away to save her from her own foolish ambitions.

Clearly lies. Every last one.

It struck her how amazing one's ability to create false ideas about another person's thoughts and intentions was. Even when you thought you knew them. Seemed worse, in fact, the more you knew the other person. Like she presumed she knew his every thought, when really, all she'd done was assume the worst of him.

Turned out, the worst wasn't all true.

Hunter munched at his burnt meal as the silence lengthened. Janie wondered if it would be possible to bridge the distance they'd blasted between them—and found herself amazed that she hoped it would be so.

Did he?

She peeked at him. "Hunter?"

He brushed the crumbs from his hand. "Yeah." His gaze captured hers again. Open. Hopeful?

Did she dare ask?

She cleared her throat. "I uh . . ." She wasn't that brave. Not yet. "What are you doing here?" She nodded back at the trailer Hunter now claimed as home. "With that, I mean."

"I told you. Living."

"Why in a trailer?" Staring at her hands, she knotted her fingers together. "And why this spot?"

"It's a good spot." He paused, and Janie noted that the cavalier *you're not touching my heart* tone had disappeared. His next statement came out in full earnestness. "I have good memories here."

Sucking in a breath, she dared to look at him. Warmth and quiet pain seeped through his steady gaze. This place was still sacred to him. And he still counted those memories as good, even if the things that had followed weren't.

Janie ran her thumb along her left fourth finger. Sometimes she could still feel the cool metal of that thin band. And in that moment, she allowed the clear memory of Hunter giving it to her to replay in her mind.

Right there—just in the distance near enough to the veil of falling water that the light spray had kissed her cheeks. He'd knelt against the damp earth, taken her hand, and asked her to wait for him. He'd promised to come back after college and marry her. If she said yes.

And she had. It had been more of a giddy squeal. An enthusiastic, heartfelt-all-the-way-to-her-toes *yes* if there ever was one.

Squeezing her eyes shut, Janie willed back the burn of tears as she felt the weighty absence of that ring on her finger. It'd been so long since she'd slipped it off and given it back to him, she shouldn't be able to still feel it there as if it'd been taken off an hour before.

"Janie."

With a flutter of lashes and a realignment of her shoulders, she looked at him again.

"Can I tell something?"

"Yes," she whispered.

"I didn't come here aimlessly, because I have nothing else going. I have a plan. It's a good plan—Bennett even said so."

"A plan . . ."

"Hazel is going to hate it though."

Her heart stalled as she suddenly understood what was happening. He was putting her in the middle. Just like Hazel had. She'd often been in the middle of the Wallace siblings, and it was never comfortable. The pair of them . . . couldn't they just talk things out themselves without having a mediator all the stupid time?

Janie held up a hand. "I'm not your fix-it girl anymore, Hunter. Fight your own battles."

"Is that what you told Hazel when she sent you here to find out what I was up to?"

"Wha—"

"As if I couldn't guess." He crossed his arms and tipped his head to one side. "Don't play coy, Janie—you're terrible at it."

She mashed her lips together and shook her head. "You two are both children. You know that?"

He shrugged. "Here's the thing—I need you."

The beating in her chest stalled as her stomach clenched. "You—"

"Back me on this. I need you to do that. Please?"

"I don't even know what you're talking about." Her head spun with thoughts that didn't make sense and sentiments that refused to land safely in the region of apathy bordered by bitterness. *I need you* whispered in his soft voice on delicious replay.

Hunter stood and took two steps toward the water's edge some twenty feet from his campsite. "I'm going to build a hunting lodge. A big one—a nice one. Right here." He turned back, pinning her with a demanding look that didn't match the tender words still reeling through her mind. "It's my land too. I need you to get that through to Hazel."

And there was reality again. He didn't *need* her, didn't *want* her. Not the way the flighty emotions that had her momentarily soaring high had interpreted things. Nope. He needed her to make sure Hazel didn't march over, bringing him a shovel, and watch him dig his own grave.

Had he ever needed her, wanted her, just for *her*?

Ugh. She was so unbelievably gullible. With a huff, Janie stood. "You're a big boy, Hunter. Solve your own problems."

She'd not made it five steps back up the path before his jog caught up with her stomping strides. One large hand curled around hers, and he pulled her to a stop. Then he spun her around, and suddenly she was staring at his chest.

Scowling, she tipped her chin so she could fire her glare straight at his face. His was already pinned on her. And there they stood. Horns locked, stares unwavering.

Hearts hammering.

Time fading.

Heads swimming.

Lines blurring.

The fingers that had held tight around her fist loosened, and then they wove with hers. She was breathing, right? Why did her body feel like when she'd gone through a half a bottle of wild strawberry wine a little too fast? Did the space between them narrow? When did he lean down so that his nose nearly brushed hers?

The sweet, heady soaring sensation returned in double portion. She was flying, falling . . . reaching for something to steady herself, she found the sleeve of his T-shirt and rolled her fingers into it.

"Janie. . ." When he whispered her name, she couldn't help the slipping of her eyelids shut. "Be on my side." His forehead nestled against hers. "Please?"

Suddenly she wanted to sob. At one point, all she had wanted was to be on his side. At his side. Right there, next to his heart forever and ever amen. This wasn't fair.

Blinking, she stepped back, releasing her grip on his shirt, and made herself rigid again. "Don't manipulate me," she whispered.

His lips parted and eyes widened as if she'd slapped him. "I'm not."

"You are." She sucked in a fortifying breath. Then she scowled as anger became the lead weight she needed to end this flighty reaction. "You are, and I resent you for it. If you want a life here, that's fine. It is your land too, and you have a right to it just as much as Hazel does. But don't put me in the middle. And don't—" Her voice wobbled. She cleared her throat, jerking her fingers from his hold. "Don't toy with my heart anymore. You already broke it once. You don't get another chance."

With that, she turned on her heel and marched to her Jeep. The hand that he'd held felt cold and empty. Just as it had the day she'd given him back that ring.

Seventeen

Hazel leaned back against the smooth boards of the Adirondack chair, a deep sigh escaping her chest. She shut her eyes and tipped her head back, angling her face to catch the warming rays of the morning sun. While Ice and Cream made their morning rounds investigating the horse corral, the tack shed, the shack, and the trail leading around the lake, Scout rested her chin on Hazel's knee, waiting with stubborn patience for Hazel to scratch her ears.

Absent-mindedly, she did. The dog leaned into Hazel's leg and then laid on her foot, Scout's tongue moving to the rhythm of her steady panting.

Allowing her weight to sag, which destroyed her usual strong posture, Hazel sighed. Weariness cloaked her this morning. Several nights of not sleeping well would do that to anyone. As Hazel was used to sleeping like a rock on the north side of the ridge, *not* sleeping well was wrecking her. A foggy sensation made her throbbing head feel heavy, and she considered taking an early morning nap right there in the golden sun.

Hazel never took naps. Dang it, Bennett.

The low growl came from her throat, not Scout's.

On one hand, if Bennett hadn't insisted on sleeping in the bunk room again, she might have found more rest. On the other hand, if he hadn't, she might have kicked him out and made him sleep there anyway. The traitor.

Relationships were complicated. Why did it have to be so stinking hard? She knew she loved him. Believed Bennett when he said he loved her. Except for now he'd drawn a line. Taken a step back.

Did he love her?

Hazel didn't get it, and his retreat made her feel like she was in a freefall.

All that aside, she was dang mad at him about his helping Hunter with the trash-can trailer, and she didn't have any plans to get over it anytime soon.

Breathing in deeply, Hazel shut her eyes and focused on the crisp smell of the mountain lake, the sweet scent of wafting pine, and the earthy tones of the damp shoreline. Exhaling slowly, she leaned forward and rolled her head one way and then the other. Perhaps if the tightness in her neck would loosen, the annoying throb of her head would cease. That would help her mood.

At her feet, Scout perked her head up and let out a curious squeak. Hazel bent and gave Scout another head pat, then leaned back against the chair again. Apparently satisfied that Hazel was well, the pup settled her chin back against her paws.

Next to Hazel, the other chair remained empty. Surely Bennett was up by now?

Rather than looking back at the cabin for her boyfriend, Hazel let her study travel over the dark stain of the treated wood—exactly what she would have chosen if she'd picked it out herself. She hadn't—the Adirondack set had been a gift from Bennett. He'd brought it up with him a month before, and she'd been thrilled.

He was thoughtful like that. And so kind to her, even when she was being a badger—which she hated to admit was way more often than she'd realized. Bennett was a patient man. He was a funny man. He was a gentle man.

Bennett was the only man who could have cracked the lock on her heart. A thing for which she was in splendid awe of and at the same time uncomfortable with.

Even so, he had a way of making her mad. So, so mad. And confused. Both of which caused her to lose sleep. And that was why she sat there alone, exhausted and discontented.

The sound of feet stepping onto the other end of the dock at her back brought her attention around. There was the man himself, carrying two mugs of steaming coffee—his brew, because he wouldn't drink her instant "garbage"—and at his side lumbered her Great Pyrenees, Moose.

Another traitor. Contrary to the substance of that thought, it tickled the slightest grin against the corner of her mouth.

Basically, Moose was Bennett's dog now. Or Bennett was Moose's person. It was hard to tell which. The big dog moped around when Bennett was in Bozeman, and Bennett inevitably ended up on the ground playing with Moose upon arrival at Elk Canyon. Hazel often had to wait her turn for a greeting.

She snorted a soft laugh as she remembered the first time Bennett had frozen stiff at his first glimpse of the massive dog. He'd sure come a long way.

They both had.

As dog and man neared, Bennett's attention narrowed on her and he lifted a weak smile. Stopping at her side, he leaned down, slid a mug on the arm of her chair, and kissed her temple. "Morning, beautiful."

Pleasure rebelliously oozed from her chest. How was she supposed to confront him with convincing anger when he started the day with a fresh hot brew and *morning, beautiful*?

Did he mean to make her putty?

Bennett lowered onto the other chair, took a sip of his special brew—which admittedly was significantly better than her dehydrated granular stuff—and settled back against the semi-reclined chair. "Have I told you this view is amazing?"

"You might have mentioned it a time or two." He had. Every time he'd stayed up there. That was well over two dozen times by now—more than enough to make her feel his absence when he wasn't there.

"I'll never get over it." He reached for her hand.

She toyed with his fingers, not taking a committed hold. "I'm still mad at you."

A stifled sigh slipped from his lips before he wrangled up another weak grin, lifted her knuckles to kiss them, and then released her hand. "I know."

"That's all you're going to say?"

His chin came around slowly, and when he settled his gaze against hers, she read mild frustration in those blue eyes. "I'm not sorry, Hazel, if that's what you're expecting from me. I mean, I'm sorry that you're mad at me about it, and I'm sorry that there are things between us that we don't agree on. But I'm not sorry that I helped your brother. In fact, if you want the full truth, I'm frustrated that you're being a bit of a child about this."

Hazel flinched and sat back. "What?"

"You keep saying things like 'What is he doing here?' And 'Why the heck did he move that trash can onto my land?' As if Hunter doesn't have any right to be here at all. Do you hear yourself, Zel? Do you hear how selfish that sounds?"

Clamping her jaw tight, Hazel fought against the trembling that started in her core. "I don't think I want to hear this first thing in the morning."

"I don't want to say it first thing in the morning. Or ever. I'm really tired of being at odds with you. I miss our long walks minus conflict and easy laughs and moonlit fishing. But this is life, and we're not always going to float on easy romance." Slumping back against the chair, he scrubbed one palm across the unshaved stubble of his jaw. "And the truth is, you *need* to hear this."

The crisp morning air crackled between them as a songbird sang awkwardly into their tension. Why were men given to this . . . overbearing, condescending . . . whatever.

The Facebook universe called it toxic masculinity. Was that what this was? Bennett being . . . toxic?

Hazel's mind slammed against that with a hard thunk. She didn't know a whole lot about the world beyond Elk Canyon, but she'd had enough exposure to the bizarre chaos that was social media to know not to buy in to that nonsense.

Especially when she knew—even if she didn't care to say it—that Bennett might have a point. Hearing her words echoed back to her made her cringe.

She'd been pretty selfish. Even Janie had hinted so.

Finally Bennett sat forward and swiveled his body until he was perched uncomfortably on the edge of his chair. He claimed her hand again, sandwiching it between both of his. His tone softened from sharp rebuke to mild pleading. "Hazel, you're a better person than this."

"Maybe I'm not," she bit. "I did trick you when you couldn't remember who you were."

A low growl emanated from his chest, and he slid his touch from her. "You are some kind of stubborn, I'll give you that." Then he scooted to stand. To leave.

Panic kicked in her chest. If he walked down that dock, would he just keep right on going? How long was he going to put up with her little fit? Maybe he was right. She was acting like a child. Truth was, she wasn't entirely sure how to act otherwise about this.

Hazel was utterly unpracticed at putting someone else before herself. She'd lived alone most of her life, and when she didn't, Hunter had pretty much seen to her every whim.

Her brother had spoiled her.

And now she was behaving like Hunter was enemy number one? Bennett definitely had a point.

Hazel stood the same moment Bennett pushed up to his feet. Scout popped up from her sprawled-out position on the dock, her tail whipping around with excitement, as she clearly thought they were going for a hike. A *long walk minus conflict* sounded nice right then. Hazel held her hand out to the dog in the *sit* hand signal, then met Bennett's disappointment with penitence. "Don't leave."

His shoulders slumped, and he bent down to scratch Scout's head. "I don't know what to do when you're like this. Everything I say makes you madder. But, Hazel"—he stood straight and crossed his arms, locking his gaze with hers—"I'm going to do what I think is right, even if you don't like it. That's just how it is."

She swallowed. He wasn't just talking about Hunter now but making a reference to his choosing the bunk room over sharing her bed these past two visits. The pressure of her frustration mixing with fear built again. Biting her bottom lip, she weighed carefully how to proceed.

"I'm sorry I disappoint you," she whispered.

He groaned and then reached to take her shoulders in a gentle hold. "Only with this situation with Hunter." He dipped lower to make eye contact. "Let's be clear on that, okay?"

So they were keeping to only the *one* topic. Probably better that way. Hazel swallowed.

"Zel, he's your brother and the only family you have left right now. And I know he matters a whole lot to you, even if you're too stubborn to admit it."

Slowly she nodded.

"And . . ."

His hesitation caused her to lift her brows, partly wondering how far he was going to take this lecture and partly warning him not to go wherever he was intending to go. Because she was certain she wasn't going to like it, and it wasn't going to make things better.

Bennett didn't flinch at her silent warning. ". . . this land is his too. I've seen the papers—he sent them to me last year before I even agreed to come and look at the place. I told him it was a nonstarter if he didn't have legal claim to it. He does. You're joint inheritors, joint owners."

The pulse in her ears drummed as heat climbed up her neck. "You . . . you've looked into my property?"

"That shouldn't surprise you, Zel. You know where we started, why I came up here in the first place. Let's not move backward. The point is, this is his place just as much as yours. He has a right to live here. To try to make a life here. Every bit as much as you do."

Hazel's emotions slid right back into the furious zone. Bennett must have expected so, because he slipped his hands from her shoulders and backed away.

The moment felt like a test. Was he putting her to the test? Would Bennett do such a thing? And if she chose to cling to fury, give him the cold shoulder, and walk away . . . then what?

Then she'd be acting like a child, just as he'd said. How long was he willing to put up with that? And was she willing to risk losing his respect—maybe losing *him* entirely—just to vent her emotions?

Rolling her fists, Hazel squeezed her eyes shut and reached out to an unknown *Something* to ask for help—to be the better person Bennett claimed she was.

Ugh! Relationships! No wonder Pop had spent most of his life wandering the woods on his own. A tangled ball of fitfulness bounced around in Hazel's mind as she tried to put herself toward being an unselfish adult rather than a petulant child.

"Just try, Zel."

Anger won. Her chin snapped up, and she crossed her arms. "Like you try with your dad?"

A flash of heated pain streaked through Bennett's gaze before he stepped back and rubbed his neck.

Ah. Same shoe, different foot.

Bennett's jaw worked, and then his Adam's apple bobbed. And after another heartbeat, so did his head. "You're right," he said quietly.

Wait . . . she was? She didn't expect him to just . . . agree. More like she'd hoped he wouldn't and then they could both stay on the mad side of their hard relationships and not challenge each other to deal better with them.

Bennett drew in a long breath and let it go slowly, then regained the space he'd opened between them and reached toward her. The softest graze of his fingertips trailed down the length of her arm. "You're right. I haven't done well with my dad or his family. It's time I try again." He tipped his head and lowered it to meet her gaze. "It's time we both try."

"I don't know how." The words tumbled from her mouth before she could filter them.

He stepped closer still, and both his hands clasped hers. A relief. She looked up at him.

"Accept this." Bennett shook his head. "*Embrace* it, Zel. You have your brother back, and he's not going to try to sell Elk Canyon. Those are both *good* things. Start with that."

The truth of what he said seemed to dump on her like an avalanche. She'd been so mad at Hunter for leaving, and now he was home. She'd been terrified he'd sell out from under her, and now he wanted to make a life there.

Those were good things. They were incredible things. She bit her bottom lip against the enormity of emotion that provoked. In the space of a heartbeat, Bennett's arms were around her, pulling her snug against his chest.

Hazel snaked her arms around him and held on. "I don't know why it's so hard . . ."

For several minutes, they simply held there.

"What will you do?" she asked into the comforting steadiness of his heart beating against her cheek.

The muscles of Bennett's back tensed. "Go see him. Them."

He was serious about it then? That was a big deal. Up until last Christmas, Bennett hadn't talked to his father in years. He'd only met his stepsiblings a handful of times, and never by choice.

Hazel curled her grip on Bennett's shoulder, and his hold around her tightened. The rhythm of his heart picked up. What had she pushed him into? Should she volunteer to go with him?

No way. She wasn't that kind of woman, even if it did mean she was selfish.

Scout dropped to the wood planks of the dock, laying her head on her paws, as if she knew this was going to take forever. Moose made an approving sound and rolled to his side to enjoy the morning sun. All was right with their worlds.

Hazel wanted to believe all was right with hers too. Shouldn't be hard to imagine—just the small issue of their relationship being a maze and their family dynamics being a wreck.

Bracing her head against him, she shut her eyes.

She'd never clung to anyone in any measure—except perhaps to her brother for a few years. Now she lived in fear that somehow she'd ruin this bizarrely wonderful thing she'd stumbled into with Bennett. She'd lose this man. After all, she had no real idea how she'd managed to slip into his heart in the first place. If she believed in miracles, she'd name it that.

And maybe it was.

But perhaps miracles were revokable. Maybe love was retractable.

Bennett rubbed her back and then eased away, though he regained his grip on her hands. "Let's go do something fun, hmm?"

Thank the big blue Montana sky for a reprieve. She'd take it with both hands and a foot, thank you very much.

"What did you have in mind?"

He shrugged. "Show me something amazing. Someplace I haven't seen yet."

Ah, this. For a city boy scared of the big sky of this vast wilderness and the unnerving quiet and the unfamiliar ways of nature, Bennett had become quite the outdoorsman—even if he still wasn't entirely comfortable with the dark. He'd hike with her for hours. Sit in the brush just to take in the view. Snap pictures with a real camera that he'd acquired earlier that year. He'd even trekked with her on a spring turkey hunt—sans a gun because he still didn't like them.

Hazel suspected that his efforts in nature were a whole lot for her, but maybe he truly enjoyed the outdoors for himself too. She hoped so.

"Are you up for riding a horse?"

He squeezed her hands. "I've been practicing."

"You have? Where?"

"A friend I made playing racquetball—I mentioned him to you. José." He turned, grabbed his mug from the arm of the chair, and then led her down the dock toward the cabin. "He goes to my church, and his family ranches just outside of Bozeman. His sister has been giving me lessons."

Hazel stopped, shooting a furrowed look at him. "His sister?"

Bennett tucked her under his arm. "Don't do that. I'm in love with *you*. I've made no secret of it." He kissed the top of her head. "You have nothing to worry about."

They reached the front porch of the cabin, and he took the half-drunk mug from her hand and then clamored up the steps to put both mugs in the kitchen. When he reappeared on the decking, Hazel followed his progress back down the steps. "How long have you been taking lessons?"

"A few of weeks—just on Sunday afternoons when I'm there."

"You didn't say."

"Surprise." He winked and kept going toward the small run-in shed and corral.

"I'm not sure I like that surprise."

"Hazel." He waited, arm stretched over the wood crossbeam of the corral fence.

She continued forward until she was in front of him.

"Let's have a good day together." He cupped her jaw and ran the pad of his thumb over her cheekbone.

"You love me?" She felt so insecure these days. Like this relationship had ripped off all the false pretense of her being entirely self-confident and independent. Were relationships supposed to do that? It was stupid and annoying, and most poignantly, the truth.

Bennett leaned down and pressed his lips to hers. When she slipped closer, he pulled her in and let the kiss grow more intimate. A soft sigh that might have been more of a groan slipped from her throat. Hazel's heart raced as she kissed him back. All of her stiving against fear and frustration quieted. The swirling thoughts about possibly losing him and how different they were and how much she didn't understand him fell into a silent abyss. There in his arms, his breath mixed with hers, it was as if her heart found the peace and home she'd been unknowingly searching for her whole life.

He was hers, and she was his, and it was more beautiful than all the wonders she so dearly loved in Elk Canyon.

By the time he pulled away, they were both breathless.

"I love you," he whispered.

For that moment, she believed him, and it felt like security.

Eighteen

Bennett breathed in deep as he climbed up the steep trail of loose dirt and large boulders. They'd left the horses loosely tethered a half-mile back, where the trail had changed from a little scary to steep and terrifying. Though his heart thudded so hard that his pulse thumped in his ears, he could happily claim that the struggle wasn't nearly as much on this hike as it would have been five months before. Man, between the altitude and his lack experience in snowshoeing, he sure had struggled the first few times Hazel had taken him out in her vast wilderness she claimed as home.

That day they didn't need the added challenge of snowshoes, and he had the advantage of practice and acclimatization. Added to it, he still had the driving desire to impress this fierce, quirky woman who seemed to be part mountain lion and part lamb.

He'd not been impressing her much lately. At that pesky thought, Bennett blew out a breath.

"Need a breather?" Hazel paused her steady pace and turned to check on him.

"No, I'm doing okay." He winked. "Look at me, almost a mountain man."

She smiled. Warm and sincere and so lovely. His head felt suddenly light. Hazel Wallace was the best high he'd ever known, and he intended to keep it that way.

Oh man, he loved that smile. Made his heart drop and adrenaline zip through his veins. He sure wished he could always gain that response from her, rather than the scowls he'd become proficient in earning lately.

Were relationships always this much yo-yoing? He'd supposed so—after all, there had to be a reason the divorce rate was so high. This being-in-love-and-staying-committed business was not for the weak.

Bennett had enough weakness in his life. And he sure didn't want to replicate his father's life.

His father . . .

He swallowed hard as a knot pulled tight in his chest.

"We're nearly there." Hazel pointed toward an outcropping of black rocks at the top of this rise—a landmark Bennett couldn't see twenty minutes ago. "And this levels off quite a bit here in about fifty feet."

"Perfect." Packing those worrisome nigglings about his dad away to deal with later, he climbed the five feet of distance separating them and then reached for her hand.

Hazel squeezed his fingers and turned to continue upward.

She'd been right. The faint trail leveled into a much easier walk in less than the length of a football field. At that point, the footpath disappeared entirely.

"Where'd the trail go?"

"There isn't one."

"Why?"

"I usually turn around back there, and the game don't go this way. It's too exposed."

"Why do you turn around before you get to the top?"

Hazel glanced at him, her eyes a telling green—though mossy and not bright—and then continued toward the outcropping. Her grip on his hand firmed, and the shoulders she typically kept straight rounded.

Timidity seemed to swallow her entire demeanor as they neared the outcropping of dark granite.

Once there, Bennett pulled in a sharp breath. "Wow."

On the other side was a sheer drop. The ravine below was narrow and at least two hundred feet down. Cold air climbed up the rock face and blasted against Bennett's exposed skin, a welcome relief to the warm sweat he'd worked up on the climb. The view at his feet was startling, if not magnificent. He trembled as he leaned to peer down the ledge.

The woman at his side clung to his arm, hung back from the edge, and remained stiffly silent.

Not normal.

Bennett shifted his awestruck stare from the stunning—and unnerving—drop at his feet to study Hazel. Before they had set off on this trail, she'd slipped that wide scarf-headband thing over her hair, but her honey-blond braid rested against her shoulder, the loose wisps of escaped hair dancing in the chilly breeze. Her face was white, and her eyes focused on her feet, not on the enormous view just beyond her boots.

Hazel looked terrified.

"Zel?" Bennett stepped back from the edge until the drop was no longer in view. Clinging to his arm, she moved backward with him.

He was the one afraid of heights—not her. She loved everything wild and gloriously too big and unnerving.

Turning to square with her, Bennett nudged her chin to tip her face up. "What's going on?"

She swallowed, and her eyes glanced toward the sudden canyon before reconnecting with his. "This is where they died."

"They . . ."

"My parents." She gestured with her chin. "They died on that climb."

Bennett's lips parted, but he didn't let a sound escape. They'd only talked about her parents a handful of times—Hazel never wanted to get into it. She'd only told him that they were both extreme adventurers and had died in a sudden storm while out on a climb. She'd been twelve, Hunter nearly fifteen.

"A storm came in fast and strong. They couldn't see. Pops said Dad should have known better . . ." She winced. Years of pain and confusion unveiled in that look. "Hunt says Dad *did* know what he was doing. So did Mom. Neither were at fault. It was just one of those freak accidents."

Bennett eyed the drop again. Did they *fall*? Man . . . "Do you remember any of it?"

She shook her head. "I was old enough to, but all I really remember is that there was a helicopter, but nothing could be done, and that they were cremated, and we scattered their ashes up here. Over there." She pointed to the spot where the trail had abruptly disappeared. "And that my grandparents were never the same again. Especially Pops."

Bennett nodded, silently processing. Why had she decided to bring him here? There had to be some kind of connection . . .

"What about Hunter? Did he change?"

She nodded. "He was . . . Usually he was my champion. He made sure I was okay. When some people from the state tried to rehome us because Nan and Pops were so remote, he somehow made sure that didn't happen. I don't know what he did or said, but he got me back home. But sometimes . . ." She trailed off and looked down at the fingers she was knitting together.

"Sometimes?"

Shrugging, she let her shoulders sag. "Sometimes he lost it."

"Lost it . . . how?" Bennett's pulse ramped up. "Was he violent?"

Hazel shook her head. "No."

Bennett felt his jaw jump, and something feral awakened within. If he found out that Hunter had . . . No. Hazel said he hadn't been violent. But what then? "Help me understand."

"He just . . . wasn't okay. I don't know what else to say. There were things that he did—I couldn't understand them."

Rolling his fists, Bennett glanced over his shoulder, back down the mountain, toward the lakes and then turned back to take Hazel by the shoulders. "Did he hurt you, Zel?"

"No," she whispered. She blinked, clearly annoyed at the moisture sheening her eyes. "I don't know why I brought you here. Why I told you."

That stung. He wanted her to tell him everything. To trust him with everything. Maybe he'd finally understand her complex and sometimes infuriating way of handling life. Specifically, Hunter. Maybe he'd figure out how to better respond to her.

"You love your brother." He tried to piece it together.

"Yes."

"But you're still mad at him for things that happened back then."

"Yes."

"But I don't need to go beat him?"

She snorted a soft, almost teary laugh. "No." Finally she looked into his eyes again. "But thanks for the offer. I just wanted you to know—to understand—that things are complicated. Hunter looked out for me. But sometimes . . ."

"Sometimes he let you down."

Biting her lip, she nodded.

"And now you're really afraid he'll let you down again."

Again, she nodded.

He got that. Boy, did he ever understand that—it was the runner-up reason that he still hadn't mended bridges with his dad, coming in right behind the defeating fact that he was still—after all these stupid wasted years—mad at his father.

God, we're both such broken messes. Do we even have a real chance together when we're so broken all by ourselves?

The prayer felt desperate and empty.

Feeling like he was on a very narrow ledge, Bennett reached for her and tucked her in close. He hated that she had this ache lodged in her heart. Wanted to make the hurt and the resentment go away. But there was this reality he was keenly aware of.

People let people down. *He* let people down—the people who mattered most to him. He'd let them down.

Just like his dad had let him down.

That was the hard, sad reality of life. People messed up. Relationships were messy. Forgiveness was hard.

Bennett had had to come to terms with that with his dad, more now than ever, and it was hard.

Hazel needed to reconcile things with her brother. They both needed it—because whatever barbs were still lodged between them were toxic and painful, and the wounds infected every other relationship the siblings had.

A verse from Psalms leaked into Bennett's mind, carried by the gentle sound of his mother's voice. *He reached down from on high and took hold of me; He drew me out of deep waters.*

That had been Mom's testimony to him—her proclamation of God's faithful goodness to her even while she had almost drowned in her anger and pain after Dad had left her. God had drawn her out of the deep waters that churned with something near hate, and He had given her the strength to forgive. And then to live.

Wasn't that what they all wanted? Needed? He and Hazel and Hunter and Janie? All of this striving and struggle with each other and with the different circumstances in life that kicked them sideways—wasn't it the fierce fight to truly *live*?

And love.

Bennett drew in a long, deep breath and tried not to let it shudder as he exhaled. The future seemed precarious indeed.

Sooner or later he would let Hazel down—and she would let him down. Given that they both had a tremendously hard time forgiving and reconciling with those who had disappointed them in the past—with people who were important to them—how would they get through the inevitable disappointment in each other in the future?

He might find out real quick, because he still hadn't told her Hunter's plans for the lodge. Man, that was going to be grueling.

But not a thing for this moment.

Bennett tightened his hold around her. "I'm sorry you lost your parents."

Pressing her head into his chest, she sagged against him. Bennett savored the comfort of her weight pressing into him.

One day at a time. One issue at a time. Right now she'd gifted him with a measure of her trust by bringing him there. By offering him this small sliver of her heart. Even if was from a painful place in her past, he treasured that.

Shutting his eyes, he held her close and laid his head atop hers.

Draw us out of deep waters. Please, Father. Draw us out . . . let us live.

And love.

Together.

Nineteen

It was *so* quiet.

Hunter stared out over the lake, mesmerized by the tiny ringlets that spread to wide circles on the surface of the steely water, all made by bugs dipping in for a drink. The day had been comfortably warm, meaning he'd shed his navy sweatshirt somewhere around two. He'd spent the day clearing saplings from his envisioned lodge footprint with a pair of long pruners he'd acquired from Mama Bulldog's store earlier that week. Now, with hands sore from holding the handles all day and biceps aching from the constant clipping motion, he sat back against that untrustworthy sling chair and watched while evening claimed the area yet again.

Man, it was so quiet. Not silent, but quiet. He'd forgotten that about Elk Canyon, but now as he sipped a mug of steaming decaf and let his mind wander backward in time, he remembered how loud city life had seemed his first year away from home. The traffic, the sirens, the constant motion . . . never stopped. It had all made sleeping difficult and seemed to have caused his normal pulse rate to increase.

Curious about that, Hunter found the thudding rhythm on his neck and turned his smartwatch to watch the seconds go by while he counted the beats.

Eleven in ten seconds. That made sixty-six.

He dug out his cell phone from his jeans pocket and swiped through the apps until he found his fitness tracker. There, he scrolled until he found his normal resting heart rate from the previous six months.

Seventy-eight.

Maybe there was something to this quietness.

Curious if he'd messed up his count, Hunter repeated the process.

"Are you having a heart attack?"

Startled by Hazel's voice coming from behind him, Hunter sat forward and swiveled around. His phone tumbled to the ground, thankfully landing in the pine needle–cushioned dirt rather than on a rock.

He blew out a dramatic breath. "I might be now. Sheesh, Zel. Let a guy know you're there, huh?"

Wandering toward his little campfire setup, Hazel gave him a wry smile. "I'm a Wallace. We only do stealth."

True. They had their grandfather to thank for that.

When she reached the edge of his outdoor dining room/kitchen, Hunter sat back and motioned to the sling chair folded up and lying on the ground nearby. "There's a chair there, if you want it. Can't promise that it'll hold though."

Hazel spared him a peek—a look that told him she was relieved and maybe a little surprised that he welcomed her to his domain—and then set up her seat a little ways from him. When she sat, she was facing more the lake than him. But that wasn't an insult. The view, as Bennett had said, was stunning.

The dwindling campfire bounced with oranges and yellows, an occasional snap popping from the burning pine. Somewhere near the shoreline, the splash of water proclaimed the presence of trout—one who just nabbed his dinner from the surface of the water.

No rush of traffic. No shouts of kids banging in and out of apartments, nor the back-and-forth of the couple who lived three apartments down and likely should not be together, given their constant fighting.

It was so quiet. And there sat Hazel, blending in with the quiet.

He hadn't seen her in five days, and the last time they'd spoken, she'd called him an impulsive idiot for buying his camper. For the record, he was neither impulsive nor stupid, but Hazel might never acknowledge that fact.

Hunter crossed his arms and watched his sister with a sideways look. Her hair hung across one shoulder in a loose braid—her normal style, though she wasn't wearing a hat or a headband like she typically would. At least, Hunter thought that was typical. It was what he'd seen her do on his sparse visits. Her shoulders were square in her straight posture, though she didn't seem tense. Just . . . strong, even with her petite, willowy frame.

Strong. Stubborn. Independent. Hazel was all of those in spades. Hunter was shocked to see her there—most cases it would be him to cave, to try to breach whatever fallout they'd had.

"Did curiosity overcome you?" he asked.

With a glance, Hazel shrugged. "A little, I guess."

Hunter motioned to his new home. "What do you think of my castle?"

"I already told you what I thought."

"Huh." Shaking his head, he snorted. "Sort of thought you'd be a little softer since you wandered all the way over the ridge just to see it."

"Bennett says I should give you a chance with this." She waved a hand toward his home.

"I see . . ." Had Bennett talked to her about the other, way bigger and more explosive thing?

Hazel sat back, relaxing that strong posture. "So here I am. Giving you the benefit of the doubt—even if I still don't understand why you would choose to live in a trash can rather than a perfectly good cabin." She shook her head, and then a grin broke over her way-too serious face. "Idiot."

At her teasing tone, Hunter chuckled. "Mule."

Guess Bennett hadn't broached the lodge topic yet. Maybe that was wise. They could ease her into this.

Hazel shifted to dig into her jacket pocket, then tossed a nearly frozen twinkie to him. Hunter caught it, but just barely for the suddenness of it. A slow grin lifted his mouth as he examined the treat. Days long past, when they'd made the trek down to Luna and were met by Mama Bulldog and a twinkie for each of them, flashed through his mind. *See, there was good back then . . .*

Hunter ripped open the plastic and held the cake to his nose to inhale. "Someone's been to town recently, hmm?"

"Nope. Bennett brings them."

"He does? Seems a little unhealthy, not to mention cheap, for the guy I remember."

"Yeah. He calls them my junk fetish, but once he discovered I love them when we were out on Navy Pier one night, he started bringing them on his visits. For the record, though, he loves hot dogs, so there is that."

Hunter tried to picture his backwoods, hunting, fishing, and living-off-the-land little sister on Navy Pier in Chicago. That was a stretch too far for his imagination. Then he tried to picture Bennett devouring a hot dog. Easier than imagining his college buddy on a big-game hunt, but not by much.

Life was full of unexpected twists.

"Everyone has their weaknesses." Hunter bit into the cold spongy cake and let the frozen filling melt on his tongue. "Speaking of weaknesses, is Bennett yours, or is it the other way around?"

Ugh. Why'd he ask that? As if he really wanted to know. Actually, he did. How Bennett had fallen for the woman his friend had called a badger was one level of mystery. A whole other was how Hazel had fallen for *him*.

And were they making it work?

"You seriously want to go there?" Hazel ripped open her own unhealthy snack cake. "Because there's the thing about you going to see Janie first thing when you got back . . ."

Hunter rubbed his jaw. He decided he didn't mind that Hazel knew he still held a flame for her best friend. Everyone on the planet could know, for all he cared. What he did mind was the insinuation that it was dumb.

Even if it was dumb. Janie wasn't about to forgive him—which was particularly irritating since Hunter didn't think he was solely responsible for everything going in the dirt between them in the first place.

How in the world could Bennett and Hazel make it work when Hunter and Janie had crashed and burned in epic—and apparently eternal—flames?

"It's not a weakness," he said, somewhat to himself.

"Janie isn't?"

"Caring about someone." Something inside Hunter awakened as he continued. It felt strong, almost wild, but right. "It *isn't* weakness. Sometimes, in fact, it takes a whole lot of guts, and maybe even more determination, to care for someone." He looked straight at her and waited for her to meet his stare. "Specifically when the person you care about is unnaturally stubborn and keeps a gap about as wide as the state of Montana between you."

Yeah, he meant Janie. *And* Hazel.

Hazel dropped her gaze. With the turn of her chin, she settled her attention on the lake. And the quietness settled again.

Hunter finished his twinkie. It had been a peace offering, and maybe he'd just ruined it. That was disappointing. Man, they were a pair. Couldn't survive life without the other one, but sure had a hard time being together. Maybe because they were siblings? Or maybe because they were both broken.

They had Pops to thank for that too.

Leaning forward, Hunter stirred the dying embers of his fire. "I'm trying to say that I'm glad you have Bennett."

Was that what he was trying to say? He meant so many things. *Felt* so many things. Things that he'd run from and things that he'd longed to have back.

A relationship with his little sister was near the top of that poignant list.

"Oh." A touch of color crawled over her face. She brushed the greasy crumbs from her fingertips. "Must have gotten mixed up in the translation." Sighing, Hazel shifted in her chair, watching the gray waters of the lake. She toyed with the end of her braid and gnawed on her bottom lip.

So there they were. Doing the best they could at being together. How could they be so bad at it? They grew up together there, after all. Most days they'd really only had each other. And usually they had been a good pair back then.

Usually.

"I took him up to Black Gulch."

Jarred, Hunter jerked his attention from those weak flames of the fire to his sister. Hazel glanced his way at the same moment, and he found hesitancy in her eyes.

"You took Bennett?"

"Yes. Before he went back to Bozeman on Sunday. He wanted to take a ride. Said to take him someplace amazing."

Ride? On a horse? Bennett on a horse . . . that was bizarre. Hazel, taking Bennett to the Black Gulch . . . that was shocking. Something like panic clawed in Hunter's chest at the thought of the Black Gulch. "Do you go there often?"

"Never." She twisted her fingers together, her face tilted toward them. "Just to where we spread their ashes. And even that, not very often. Never all the way to the drop."

"But you took him all the way to the edge?" Heart hammering, Hunter tried to imagine standing there with her, peeping over the edge. Allowing the cold blast of air from the long, narrow drop to fill his lungs.

Allowing the ripping of his soul to happen all over again.

"Yes."

Hunter swallowed hard. "How was it?"

Hazel didn't answer immediately. By the movement of her jaw, she worked to swallow back her own harsh emotions. The same raw emotion that clawed at Hunter's throat.

The drop into the Black Gulch was something spectacular. Sheer faces of black granite diving straight down into a jagged debris field two hundred feet below. The view was breathtaking—horrifically so, since an ill-timed climb and a sudden storm claimed not just one of their parents' lives, but both.

There was little in this haven of Elk Canyon that terrified his little sister. The drop at Black Gulch was at the top of that short list. And conversely, as there had been a whole lot in this little entrapment of Elk Canyon that had haunted Hunter, Black Gulch topped his list.

After a long space of silence, it became apparent that Hazel wasn't going to answer his question. Which was by itself an answer.

Why had she gone there? Had Bennett asked to see it? Would Hunter have been that brave?

"I just wanted . . ." Hazel started an explanation to the questions Hunter hadn't voiced. She sounded young and vulnerable and exactly the opposite of her strong, independent self. "I wanted to somehow open myself up to him more." With the toe of her boot, she scuffed at the pine-needle litter covering the black earth. "I'm not. Open, I mean. I . . . I don't know how to be."

Interesting. And a little heartbreaking. But Hunter understood. They had never been a family of shared emotions. Connecting was a challenge all by itself, maintaining a bond . . . That was a level up neither one of them had mastered.

Was she worried about losing Bennett? Hunter put his study to her face, finding a creased brow, pulled tight above the nose. Hazel bit her bottom lip and blinked, seemingly unaware of Hunter's appraisal.

At her obvious insecurity, a severe need to protect his baby sister reemerged from the recesses of their past relationship. It had always been this way—he would see how small she was, how truly vulnerable she could be, and he would act in the best way he knew how.

Back then that had made her livid with him. Then again, back then she didn't understand he was protecting her. She hadn't known the danger, and God help him, he wanted that to remain so forever. Even if it did make her put up walls against him.

But that situation wasn't the same as this. Not by a long shot.

"Bennett says he loves you." Hunter leaned against his knees, shifting his weight in her direction.

Her face whipped to him, eyes wide.

She didn't know? "Surely he's told you so."

She nodded.

Ah, so she was surprised *he* knew. Easy enough to understand—Bennett's bold confession had thrown him off kilter too. "He even brought up marriage."

A hard swallow bobbed Hazel's neck, and her brow furrowed. She turned her face away.

Not the response Bennett would hope for, Hunter was certain. "Have you talked about it?"

She shrugged. "It's come up."

Exact same answer Bennett had given him. "And?"

A slow shake of her head sufficed for her reply.

"Zel, if you love him and he loves you, why wouldn't you want to marry him?"

"I never hoped to marry anyone." She flicked at a fly buzzing near her face. "Never saw myself like that."

"Hoped or wanted?"

She shot him a sidelong look.

Wasn't hard to know what that meant. "Bennett isn't Pops." *And Hunter wasn't Janie's dad . . .*

Man, was everyone on the planet as screwed up as the three of them?

"Pops was old. Likely he wasn't always the way he was. Nan must have had a reason for marrying him in the first place. My guess is something like blind love." Sighing, she crossed her arms. "I don't want Nan's life. I loved her, and I'm grateful to her for all she did for us. For sticking around when things weren't great—maybe there was strength in that. But I don't want to live her life." Determination made her voice hard.

Hunter resumed poking at the fire. He couldn't fault his sister for her line of thinking. Nan had shouldered hard things. Truth was, Zel didn't even know the full extent of the things Nan had endured.

But did that mean that marriage was a bad thing? A trap? Squeezing his eyes shut against the sting of smoke that a sudden breeze pushed into his face, Hunter felt a sharp stab in his gut.

He hoped not. He hoped that his grandfather's life didn't determine his. He hoped his grandmother's fate didn't dictate Hazel's.

Couldn't they hope for good things in this beautiful, haunted world they'd inherited? Couldn't they work for a better life?

Janie's bright-blue eyes holding his stare replayed in his mind, and his stomach clenched. Hunter desperately hoped for better than what had been shown to all of them. In that moment he wished that Brighton was nearer at hand. There were things Hunter could ask the older man—and his former commanding officer had a different perspective on life. The man possessed a peace about him, and a deep wisdom. Both had drawn Hunter to Brighton. Hunter had found himself craving the peace and wisdom for himself with increasing strength the more time he'd spent with the older man. The thirst for them had only intensified since he'd come home.

What if Hazel could see life differently too? Oh man, he wanted that for her every bit as much as he wanted it for himself.

There might be redemption on these shores for you too. Bennett's words, not yet even two weeks old. Hunter couldn't remember a time when he had more desperately wanted for another man to be right.

John Brighton. Bennett Crofton. Did they both hold the same secret? Could Hunter be in on it too?

Please...

"What should I do, Hunt?" Once again, his younger sister sounded nothing like herself.

Hunter looked at her, searching his heart and mind for an answer that was right and wise, wishing he could somehow channel Brighton into that moment. Though he was now closer to thirty than twenty, Hunter didn't seem to own a whole lot of wisdom. But John would know what to say...

Seek God, and you will find Him. Ah there. Parting words from Brighton before Hunter had pointed the nose of his truck north toward home.

But it didn't really have anything to do with what Hazel was asking, did it?

Please... He sent the plea heavenward again, this time with an inkling of understanding as to what he was doing with that silent cry. Praying. He was praying.

He'd never been a praying man. Never thought there was anyone listening.

But John... *and* Bennett?

The scrape of pebbles against Hazel's shoes refocused Hunter's mind. His sister stood and wandered toward the water's edge.

Hunter picked up a flat stone and followed her there. "Do you love him, Zel?" With a flick of his wrist, he flung the stone, and it skipped five times across the gunmetal-gray water.

"I... I think so." She bent to pick out her own skipping stone. "What do I know about love though?" Her toss produced seven ringlets.

She had always been competitive.

Hunter nodded. He got it—this uncertainty about love. Hadn't he messed up the love of his life, and now she could barely tolerate seeing him? He was not qualified to give relationship advice. Even so, he was Hazel's older brother, and this was a rare moment between them.

What would he want, if it was Janie asking someone like Bennett? Or John?

Seemed all Hunter wanted from the woman was for her to talk to him. Not snark at him. Not glare at him. He just wanted the words that would show him maybe her heart wasn't a locked vault where he was concerned. Wanted, with everything in him, to think that there might be a future for them even still.

And that would start with a gentle word. And some humble honesty. From them both.

"Talk to him, Hazel." Hunter rubbed his palms together.

"I talk to him all the time." Hazel flung another stone across the lake.

"No, I mean tell him the truth about how you feel about marriage. Tell him that you're afraid, and why." Hunter turned to her, gripping her elbow so that she would stop distracting herself with rocks and nature and deal with her emotions for one blasted second. "Trust him to listen and to try to understand."

"What if he doesn't?" Hazel's eyes flashed green, and then her look fell toward the shore at her toes.

"Then . . ." Then what? Hunter didn't know. "Figure it out from there, I guess."

Or . . .

Or they would end up like Janie and himself. Hopeless.

What a sad end to both of their attempts at romance.

Don't let that be her story. Hunter rolled fingers into his palms and squeezed his eyes shut. *Please.*

He was sure making a whole lot of requests for a guy who wasn't a praying man. But then again, some things in life changed.

Maybe, finally, this would be the change he'd been looking for his whole life.

Twenty

Bennett slid off the saddle with a grunt. Both hips, his backside, and the insides of his legs ached with the sort of burning pain that would keep a sane man from ever riding again.

Were men in love ever sane?

"Not bad, city boy." Isa glanced over her shoulder as she flipped the reins over her yellow horse's head and reached to free him of the headstall. She giggled softly as she turned back to slide the bit from Kipper's mouth. "You know, if you rode more than once every couple of weeks, you wouldn't hurt so much after. Your muscles would get used to it."

Get used to a saddle? As if that was a life goal he held.

Bennett was a sucker, because his muscles had screamed at him after every lesson with Isa and after the ride he'd gone on with Hazel three days before. Every experience had left him with the deep knowledge that he wanted to never do this again. Yet there he was. Taking riding lessons from José's flirty little sister. Again.

All for the love of his mountain lion of a woman. Add it to the list. Giving up his position in the lucrative company he'd built from almost nothing. Moving from a pristine condo with a lake view in downtown Chicago to a fixer-upper bungalow in the semi-wilds of Montana. Dropping everything at any time if she needed him.

No. Men in love were not sane. And he was not sorry for any of it.

Would Hazel sacrifice to be with him? The nagging vacancy in his gut provoked by that query caused him to suck in a long breath. Not that he wanted her to . . . but it was disconcerting that he doubted she would.

Isa shot a look at him again, one dark and way-too-lovely-for-her-own-good brow arched.

Bennett patted his stomach. "How does riding work up such an appetite?" Looking toward the ground, he winced. Lying wasn't a good habit to get back into. *God, it's hard to be who I want to be. Will You help me?*

"Mama makes the best tamales north of the Rio Grande. It will be worth it."

"That's more than half a country's worth of tamales." He pitched a sidelong glance at her saucy grin. "A big claim, don't you think?"

"You doubt it?"

"Not at all. Except maybe a little. I've had Rosalina's."

Isa brushed that comment aside as if swatting a fly. "Rosalina learned from Mama, so that is basically the same."

"Huh." Bennett caught the brush Isa tossed his way and smoothed the horse's sweaty hair. Seemed that riding an easy mile out and back shouldn't have worked up much of a lather, but this gray guy he'd been perched on for the past hour had sure worked one up. Come to think of it, so had Bennett. A cool breeze stirred just then, emphasizing that point as it chilled the sweat rolling down the back of his neck.

Doesn't the horse do all the work?
Yeah. Let's see how that works out for you.

The memory of that crossfire between himself and Hazel way back on day one made Bennett chuckle to himself.

"Are you laughing about the horse or about the tamales?" Isa asked over her shoulder, her hands busy grooming the big yellow guy she'd ridden. "Because either way, I'd like to know the joke."

"Nosy, aren't we?"

She shrugged. "I like jokes."

"Well, this one was on me. First time I met Hazel, she was taking me up to a lake on horseback. It was a long ride, and she asked if I'd ever ridden a horse. I said no, but how hard could it be? The horse did all the work."

Isa's head tipped back as she laughed, the tail of her thick dark braid brushing her shapely narrow waist. It was a joyous, happy sound. Unpretentious and without reins. For a moment, Bennett envied her innocent zeal for life and fun. But the next moment, he prayed José's little sister would never lose it. That she'd live under God's protection—and her brother's—and find the boundaries there had fallen for her in pleasant places.

That seemed like a wispy hope. Isa and boundaries didn't mix.

"You found out fast how wrong you were, eh?" Isa held out a palm for the brush.

Bennett passed it back. "I did."

"How on earth did a shiny-shoe guy like you end up with—what did you call her?—a mountain lioness?"

"God likes good stories, I guess." Bennett pulled up beside Isa as she strode from the corral, and together they paced easily toward the modest ranch house owned by Jorge and Marie Romero. Bennett had been there several times by this point, each of his visits feeling more and more relaxed. José and Isa's parents had an easy, welcoming way into their vibrant life.

From immigrants when José had been only a little boy, Jorge and Marie had worked and scraped and saved and worked some more until they were able to buy this ranchette on the outskirts of Bozeman. Jorge as a ranch hand and doing whatever else he could do that would pay a decent wage, and Marie as a nanny.

Just honest, determined hard work. Rags to riches looked a whole lot more like the determined ants who worked when the season was warm than it did a Cinderella fairy tale. And man, did Bennett admire them for it.

For some reason they liked him too.

A smile twitched the corner of Bennett's mouth.

Isa elbowed him. "Thinking of another good story where you look dumb that you can tell me?"

"No." Shaking his head in mock rebuke, he looked down and caught her onery grin. "Just about how much I like your family. How much I like feeling included in a small way."

"Oh." Her smile spread sincerely. "That would make Mama happy. She wants people to feel welcome in her home."

"I do."

"Thanks to me, right?"

"You are a part of it." Bennett stopped his forward motion, and Isa had to backtrack a step before she looked back up at him. He cleared his throat.

"But?"

"No but, not really." He rubbed the back of his neck. Then he motioned between them. "Only, you know that this is all just friendly and not . . ."

Her shoulders drooped. "José says I flirt too much."

Bennett held up his thumb and index finger an inch apart. "Just a tad."

Her brows raised. "Would it be different if you didn't already have a wild mountain girl?"

"Isa."

She shrugged. "It's a real question."

"It's an invalid question. I've already been pretty clear on the fact that she has my heart. That's not going to change."

For a breath, she twiddled with the end of her braid. Then she lifted her face, a bright grin back in place. "I know. Can't blame a girl though. I mean, have you seen your eyes?" She fanned her face with a dramatic flair.

Bennett shook his head. "Good grief."

"I'll bet that's what she likes most about you too." With a wink, Isa looped her arm through his and tugged him back into a walk. "No worries, city boy. I like men who like horses, anyway."

"I'm prone to say you like men, period. As in, you're boy crazy."

"Now you sound like my brother."

"He's not wrong." Bennett tugged her to a stop again. "Isa, listen. As a man who does care about you, and as someone who really values your family, what I'm trying to say is be careful."

Isa held his serious gaze for a heartbeat. Then she almost nodded. Almost. But before that action was complete, she replaced seriousness with a playful grin, tugged on Bennett's arm again, and sauntered the remaining distance to the house. "You and José worry too much. It's all harmless. I never get into trouble."

"You're young." They made it to the covered front deck, the awning a little low. Bennett ducked into the cool shadow and caught Isa's glance once last time. "And lovely, Isa. And there are men who are seared enough to take advantage of your innocent flirting." He knew all too well. He'd been one of them. "Be careful."

Dark eyes merely smiled at him, and then she turned into the house. "Mama! I brought you a hungry man!"

Oh boy. José had good reason to worry. Isa could hear just fine, but she was clearly not going to listen.

As Bennett remained outside on the deck, he prayed again for this family he'd gladly claim as his second set of kin. As he did so, his thoughts shifted toward those who were his first set. The ones he had nothing to do with. It was time to change that. After all, he had promised Hazel he would. They had promised each other they would both try.

No time like the present. Especially since he'd been putting it off for a week.

He fished his phone from his pocket and typed *Chip* into his search bar. (Yeah. Chip, not Dad. That's where they were.) He tapped twice.

The line rang.

Bennett held his breath. No going back.

Do the hard things...

It continued to ring.

His heart galloped, and a bead of sweat oozed into his hairline. Lifting his hat, he let the cool breeze tussle the matted mess, chilling the dampness against his scalp.

"Hello?"

Chest clenched. Heart stalled. Throat tightened.

"Bennett? Is that you, son?"

Clearing his throat, Bennett replaced his hat, working to quell the immediate resentment at the term *son*. "Yeah. Hey . . ." Chip? Probably not. Buddy? Not a chance. ". . . Dad."

The man on the other end of the call chuckled. "Hey. How are you?"

Some kind of mean grip clenched his neck. "I'm good."

"Everything okay?" Actual concern weighed Chip's voice.

"Uh . . . yeah." True? Bennett's head spun. He hadn't scripted this out, and he had no real clue how to plow forward. "I'm in Montana," he blurted.

"I heard that—your mom told me. That's quite a change."

"It is."

"Is she worth it?"

So Mom had told him everything. Had she told Chip the whole story—including the bizarre part of how he fell in love with a mountain lioness who had tricked him into believing they were married?

Sometimes he still wondered about his own sanity.

Bennett focused his words on the question his dad had asked. Was Hazel worth it? "Yes."

The man chuckled again. "So is this the obligatory announcement phone call?"

"Announcement?"

"You gonna seal the deal?"

Oh. Pain knifed in his chest, and the blade was double edged. One, because that was the only reason his dad thought he would call—which he had reason to believe. And two, no, this wasn't the announcement phone call. God knew Bennett wished it was.

But Hazel wasn't ready. Would she ever be ready?

"Um. I haven't proposed. We're not engaged."

"Oh." The response was surprised but not disappointed. "Sorry to jump the gun, then."

Bennett pinned his lips together. He should respond—accept that mild apology. But he didn't. He said . . . nothing. A whole, long bit of nothing.

"Benji?"

Bennett cringed. That was why he'd hated that nickname. How Hazel had found a way to make him okay with her calling him Benji, he still couldn't piece together. But she was the *only* one who was allowed to do so.

"It's Bennett, Dad."

"Oh. Right."

Another awful space of emptiness expanded.

"Do you need something, Bennett? Money or . . . advice?"

Advice? From Chip? Bennet held back a snort. Barely. Squeezing the back of his neck, he shut his eyes and then opened them to fix his gaze on the stunning Bridger Mountains.

Where does my help come from? My help comes from the Lord, maker of heaven and earth.

A much more reliable source of advice. He drank in a steady breath of crisp air. *Lord, I could sure use your help here.*

"I . . . I think that it's time we try again."

Silence answered back. In those empty beats, the fallout of their last encounter marched through Bennett's mind. Chip's unapologetic attitude. His demand that Bennett grow up and see that what was done was for the best.

Resentment threatened to climb. He worked hard to cut it down.

After several excruciating heartbeats, Bennett spoke again. "If you want to, that is."

"I do." No hesitation that time. Chip's rushed response was followed by yet another quiet laugh. The shocked kind. "I sure would like that, Bennett. Do you mean it?"

Perhaps Chip had felt bad about their last conversation after all.

"Yes." Did that count as a lie?

"Then let's do it. Can you come here?"

Flying to Chicago would take some time and effort, but that wasn't really a problem. He'd take the opportunity to visit his mom too.

"I can do that."

The fact that he had to travel back to Chicago to reconnect with his dad was the corker. Up until a few months back, Bennett had lived his whole adult life within an hour's drive of his dad's house. Of course he'd wait until he lived over a thousand miles away to make another effort.

Chip could have made the effort . . . Bennett silenced that bitter thought.

The past was done. He would make the effort. Because he'd promised Hazel he would.

No. Because it was the right thing to do. He *did* want to do the right thing.

"I suppose next week would be too soon?" Chip asked.

Dad. Not Chip. He's your dad—think of him that way. Hard to do without the residual knot of anger interfering.

Dads weren't supposed to abandon their families. They weren't supposed to traipse off to make a whole new one. And they weren't supposed to not be sorry for it.

Bennett rubbed his forehead. Man, this was hard. But he said he would.

Next week the house he was flipping would be re-sided. He'd hired a contractor but probably should be there in case anything went wrong—which it usually did. But his dad sounded so hopeful, and the longer Bennett put this off, the more likely he'd talk himself out of it. He was halfway there already.

Maybe Hunter could find his way to Bozeman for a few days to be Bennett's stand-in? If not that, he was sure José would be willing to step in should there be the need.

"Yeah, I can make next week work. Any particular reason?"

"Nathan and Gemma will be home from camp."

"Oh." Bennett tried not to sound blindsided. Why shouldn't Dad want all three of his kids together at one time? But Bennett barely knew his half brother and half sister, and they were fourteen and sixteen years younger than him.

And what about their mother? Bennett knew her well enough—she'd been the woman who had, a long time ago, been the administrator for the church where his father had pastored...

The hot ball of lingering emotions pushed harder in Bennett's chest. *Help me forgive...*

"They ask about you, you know?" Dad spoke into the pause.

"Do they?" Bennett trained his mind to focus on the present, on moving forward, which took enormous effort as the past threatened to claw him back into fury and resentment.

"Yeah. They'd like to know their big, successful brother."

Successful was a subjective concept. Yes, Bennett had a lucrative business churning back in Chicago, and he was working on making what he was building in Bozeman a go. But successful in life?

He had a whole host of regrets that would cast that label into question. One of them being shutting out his dad for so long. And ... maybe not knowing the younger siblings he had from his dad's second marriage.

Man, he was a twisted-up mess of contradicting emotions.

"It would be good to spend some time with them too." Bennett turned, giving his back to the grandeur of the mountains and catching a glimpse of José and Roselina's red Durango coming toward the ranch house on the long dirt drive.

Time to wrap this up. He couldn't deny the spiral of relief that provoked. "Let me take a look at my work schedule and then at flights, and I'll get back to you tomorrow, okay?"

"Sure. You bet. That will be great, son." Dad's enthusiasm piled higher with each phrase. "Let me know when you find flights that will work for you. I'll buy."

Bennett swatted away the irritation at his use of *son* yet again. He was Chip's son. And he was working on mending things here. He also had to squelch the irritation at the offer to cover the flight costs.

Didn't have to mean that his dad was throwing money at their non-relationship.

"Okay, Dad." That felt so odd coming off his tongue. "I'll be in touch."

"Great."

"Bye."

"Bennett?"

"Yeah."

"Thank you. This—" Dad's voice broke. "I've wanted this for a long time."

He did? Something rang distinctly false there . . .

Even so, longing rose fast and big. Didn't all sons want a relationship with their dads? Weren't they wired by God for that hope?

Bennett swallowed, finding once again that his throat had grown thick. "I know." He blinked against the burn in his eyes. "I know, Dad."

A sharp cough cut through the line. Then the clearing of his throat. "I'll talk to you tomorrow."

Nodding, Bennett rolled his free hand into a fist to stop the trembling. And then the line went dead.

That was that. He was going.

And he was terrified.

TWENTY-ONE

JANIE WIPED DOWN THE shabby-chic farm table beside the large window facing Main Street, inhaling the scent of lemon and lavender underscored by vinegar. Thursday afternoons were often slow after the lunch crowd had made an exit, and she used the time to prepare for the Friday through Sunday tourist rush. Such as it was in tiny Luna.

That could change, if Hunter's lodge was as big as she had the impression of it being. Hunter wasn't one to go into something halfway.

At the pesky thought of him—the thousandth in the space of five days since she'd visited his camp—she sighed. With the lavender-lemony cloth beneath her palm, she pressed against the table and shut her eyes.

And the moment replayed. Strong, calloused fingers woven between her own. His nose a gentle whisper against hers. His forehead against her brow. His breath a near kiss on her lips . . .

She swallowed.

Why did she keep steeping in that moment? It should make her mad—he had played her like a fiddle. Had somehow known the wick of her heart still smoldered for him and used it to manipulate her.

Had he?

The loud jingle of the bell over the café door jarred her. Sucking in a sharp breath, Janie nearly jumped straight and whirled around, pasting on a bright smile as she did.

"Good afternoon."

A middle-aged gentleman nodded and returned her greeting. "Good afternoon." He appeared fit, with a strong posture and firm shoulders, and wore a baseball cap, a gray navy sweatshirt, and a pair of dark-wash blue jeans.

Janie moved to the pine-slab service counter and scooted around it. The man sauntered behind her until he reached the counter and then sat on one of the barstools on the dining side.

"I have a little bit of pot pie left from lunch, if you're interested? Or perhaps you were looking for something sweet?"

"Pot pie sounds good. Thank you." He folded his hands and placed them on the counter. "And a lemonade, if you've got it?"

"Sure do. Be back in a jiffy." It took less than two minutes for her to retreat to her kitchen, drop her dishcloth into the sudsy cleaning bucket, wash her hands, and plate the order. With a fresh smile, she slid the pot pie and drink in front of her customer. "I always have to ask my visitors, how did you find Luna? We're kind of off the beaten path."

He chuckled. "On the map." Then he winked. "In my GPS. Because I plugged it in on purpose. I'm here to visit a friend."

"Oh yeah? Can I ask who?"

"Sure. Hunter Wallace."

Her breath sagged in her chest. "Oh." Him. Again. It was like he was one of those burs that gets tangled in your sock and then got sent through the wash. Irremovably stuck.

"Know him?"

"Yeah." She cleared her throat and then quickly added, "We pretty much know everyone around here, tiny town that Luna is."

"Ah. Of course." The man put a forkful of food into his mouth, then grunted. "This is good, miss," he said after he swallowed. He nodded, took another bite, and then nodded again. "Really good. I'll have to bring my wife next visit—she appreciates a well-made dish."

"Looks like you do too."

He chuckled, then reached across to offer his hand. "I'm John Brighton."

"Janie Truitt." They shook, and then Janie stepped back. "So how do you know Hunter?"

"I was his commanding officer down at Fallon."

"Ah, the one who dragged him to the hospital?"

"That's me."

"Thanks for doing that."

"I'm glad I found him in time. He wasn't good." A frown pulled on his mouth. Then he tapped his heart and pointed upward. "The Spirit prompted. That's all I know. And I'm sure thankful—though I am sorry to lose him as a seaman."

Janie didn't know what to say to that—to the Spirit prompting part. She believed God would do that sort of thing. Maybe. Just . . . not really in her world. Or maybe just not for her in particular. In the past five years, she and God seemed to have an ongoing cold-shoulder relationship. One that sort of mirrored what she and Hunter had. Up until a few weeks ago, she'd readily blamed Hunter for it. And maybe God too?

Now, she wasn't so sure.

"Are you and Hunter good friends?" John Brighton asked.

"Uh . . ." How to answer that? "We were close. When were younger. But we didn't really keep in touch after he left."

"Hmm."

What did that mean? Had Hunter told John about her? For some reason, she doubted it. But also maybe sort of hoped he had. Because if he had, that would mean that she'd mattered to him even while he was gone. Even in their icy silence.

Dumb thoughts. If Hunter had mentioned her, it would have been as someone he used to date. That was all. Benign. In the past. Not important now.

"Think you can help me get to him? I understand his place is remote."

"Oh." Of course that was what that *hmm* was about. Nothing whatsoever to do with her.

Help him get to Hunter? That would mean facing Hunter again. She hadn't yet dislodged the effect he'd had on her the last time. The brush of his skin against hers. The fan of his warm breath tickling her chin . . . Her middle pooled with warmth at just the brief thought of it.

It'd be best if she kept her distance.

"I'm sort of a one-woman operation here." Janie gestured toward the empty dining area. This wasn't really an excuse—it was the truth. She had the weekend rush to prepare for. Cinnamon rolls and lemon-raspberry breakfast cake. Hand pies. Her taco soup and homemade cornbread. Lots to do. "I know it doesn't look like it now, but I keep pretty busy."

John Brighton shook his fork at his nearly empty plate. "I don't doubt it." He wiped his mouth with a napkin. "No problem. I'll give Wallace a call. I'm sure we can figure it out." Pushing on the counter, he stood and dropped a twenty, then reached toward her across the counter again. "It's nice to meet you, Janie. Thanks for the lunch. Keep the change."

Generous tip. She clasped his hand a second time. "Thanks for stopping in." *And for saving Hunter's life.*

The man had pushed through the exit before Janie really considered the unspoken thought. It was sincere. She was grateful Hunter was still with them. And she wasn't sure what that meant.

That was silly. Of course she would be thankful Hunter hadn't died. That made her a not-completely-calloused human, which was a good sign, considering how angry Hunter had made her.

Picking up the cash, Janie walked it to her register, made change for the bill, and pocketed the tip. Made it easier to keep books when she kept things separate that way. Then she strode back to the kitchen to retrieve her cleaning rag.

She'd finished wiping down the dining room and the pine-slab counter, as well as every working surface in her kitchen, and was washing her hands before she started working on the yeast dough for the cinnamon rolls, when the bell above the front door jangled again. Snagging a fresh towel, she dried her hands as she reentered the retail portion of her café. The *hello, customer* smile she wore faded as the first of two men met her gaze.

"Hunter."

"Hi, Janie." Hunter waved at her with a long tube in his hand, his tone all easygoing, as if things were peachy between them and always had been.

"What are you doing here?"

"I wanted you to meet my friend. John Brighton, this is Janie Truitt."

"We met." Janie knew her tone sounded curt, but she had little to work with inside to change that. Things were absolutely *not* peachy keen between them, and in fact Hunter had made them worse the other night.

Sheesh. For the love of her sanity, and apparently her business, she *had* to stop thinking about that.

Why would Hunter want her to meet his friend? And why hadn't John Brighton told him he'd already met her?

John Brighton smiled, as if nothing was strange there. "Sure did. Fed me some outstanding grub."

Maybe nothing seemed strange to him. But Janie felt her insides squirming, as though she'd been called on in class to recite the Declaration of Independence and knew she didn't have it memorized past the first two sentences.

Yeah. That had happened. She'd been miserably embarrassed.

As though he couldn't sense her discomfort—or maybe he did and didn't care—Hunter walked right up close to her, dropped an arm around her shoulder and squeezed. "I believe it," he spoke to John. "Janie's food could haunt a man for life."

What on earth did that mean?

She shrugged from his casually draped arm and put a solid body length of space between them. "Can I help you?"

Hunter looked down at her, apparently unfazed by her intentional distance and short tone. "I was hoping you still had some Juneberry pie."

Janie controlled the urge to sigh. If only she'd sold out of that at lunch, she could say no and the pair of men would be on their way out the door. She hadn't run out, which meant they'd be sitting down. Staying. Distracting her.

Not *they*. Customers weren't a distraction. Just Hunter.

"Yes, I have a couple of slices." She worked to use her professional, cheerful voice.

"Excellent. And your cinnamon ice cream?"

She nodded. "That too."

"Two plates, then." Hunter gestured toward the center table beside the window, and the two men moved toward it. "Be sure to give Brighton a generous slice."

"Hold on that." John Brighton sat across from Hunter. "Just a sliver for me. I've barely had a chance to work off that delicious lunch."

Janie nodded and pivoted toward the kitchen. The men chatted, and Hunter opened the tube he'd brought in.

Safe in her kitchen, out of sight and unable to hear their low conversation, Janie pressed her back against the cool stainless-steel front of her oversized fridge. She pulled in a fortifying breath, held it, and let it go slowly out through her nose.

Why did Hunter possess the power to rattle her this way? Why did she still allow him that power? And what was this game he was playing at—acting like they were pals?

They were *not* pals.

Hmm. Maybe they should try to be pals. If he was going to stay in Luna and even open up a tourist business, wouldn't that be easier than . . . whatever they were currently? Is that what Hunter was doing? Trying to move forward as her pal?

Could they be pals?

She bounced her head on the fridge three times, bottling up the urge to growl. This was so dumb. Serving a couple of guys some pie shouldn't tie her up in knots.

Just serve them pie!

Obeying her command, Janie plated two slices of her Juneberry pie with a hearty scoop of her homemade cinnamon ice cream on top of each. One plate in each hand, she pushed through the swinging door with her back and delivered the order.

"Anything else?" she asked as she set the plates in front of the men.

"Yeah." Hunter looked up at her, an earnest warmth in his eyes. "You got a minute? I want to show you this too." He tapped the curling pages he'd spread between him and John Brighton.

Janie felt her brows fold in. "What is it?"

"Building plans. For the lodge I was telling you about."

She blinked. "You have plans already?"

"I told you before, Janie. I didn't come back here without a purpose. Without a plan." Hunter nodded toward the man across the table. "In fact, I discussed it thoroughly, sought wise counsel. John put me in contact with an architect. He's been helping me write a business plan. And he's here to see what I'm working with."

Janie stared at him. He sounded so . . . grown up. Responsible and reasonable and grounded.

Stunned. She was utterly stunned. Dropping onto the chair beside him, she looked at the blueprints without really seeing them. A tangle of vague thoughts rolled about in her mind, one finally taking a recognizable shape.

He came back to build a lodge. He didn't come back for me.

Pressure squeezed in her chest.

"Janie?" A hand warmed her shoulder. "Are you okay?"

Had she truly hoped that he had come back for her? Janie swallowed. Nodded. "Have you talked with Hazel about this yet?" The words came out pinched through the tightness in her throat.

The hand that had rested on her shoulder vanished. Hunter straightened and cleared his throat. "Hazel is fine."

She was? So they'd talked, and she was good with this? The dense fog that had coated her thoughts cleared away as Janie zeroed in on that claim. She turned her study to his face and saw silent pleading in his expression.

Glancing back to John Brighton, she found him watching her and Hunter. She dropped her gaze back to the plans. "Glad to hear it." She tapped the papers. "Show me."

Hunter turned into the table, and his fingers brushed her arm before he pointed out the different aspects of his building plan.

Before her was a drawing of a sprawling, two-story eight-thousand-square-foot guest house with six large suites—four upstairs and two down—an expansive dining room, an impressive industrial kitchen that made Janie nearly cry with envy, and a vaulted front room with an oversized fireplace. Massive windows would offer a view of the stunning Elk Canyon scenery—the biggest of which were in that front room and would face the minor lake. An owner's suite sat overtop of the detached four-vehicle carriage house.

She pictured the little camp and the *trash-can trailer* Hunter was currently residing in. Quite a difference.

"Is there room for this mansion?" she breathed.

"Plenty. Once it's there, you'll see it scales very well with the surroundings." Excitement underscored Hunter's words. "It will also fit in like it belongs. Timber and stone, the building itself will seem like it sprang from the hills and forest on its own."

"I very much doubt that." She also very much doubted that Hazel would approve of this once she saw it—if she even knew about it at all. Given that silent look she had understood but likely John Brighton didn't, Janie would bet Hunter wasn't being forthright about Hazel being "fine."

They would discuss that later.

"You don't think this will be awesome?" Hurt tinged his voice.

"I think it's staggering. I don't think such a massive structure could possibly look like it sprung out of the hills and forest on its own."

Hunter grinned. "I've marked out the footprint—you should come up and check it out. Maybe with John and me later?"

For several heartbeats, Janie studied him. The eager fire in his gaze. The excitement of his expression. And something else in the way he looked at her . . . Something fresh and alluring. All of it put together captivated her, and she found herself wanting this for him. "I can't come today," she stammered. "I have work to do here."

Hunter nodded as if he'd expected her to say that. Then he tapped the blueprint. "What about the kitchen?" he asked. "Do you think it'll work for a guest operation?"

Blinking, Janie shifted her attention back to the plans. "It's impressive."

"Is there enough room?"

"It's bigger than what I have here at the café. I'm sure your chef will love it." She glanced back at him. "Or were you going to learn how to cook yourself?"

He snorted. "We both know that would be a disaster."

Janie chuckled and looked at the man who had been a silent witness across from them. She shook her head as she addressed John. "He's pathetic. I wouldn't put it past him to do all of this just so he had a reason to hire someone to cook for him."

John laughed and then looked at Hunter. "If that's the case, maybe just find yourself a wife, hmm?" Then he shifted his attention back to Janie and winked.

Heat infused Janie's neck and face. She convinced herself there was no other reason for that response than the fact that the comment was rather sexist.

"That might be difficult"—Hunter didn't miss a beat—"since I very much doubt there is a woman out there who could do better than Janie."

Janie's eyes widened, and the burn in her face amped up to a full-blaze fire.

"At cooking," Hunter clarified. "No one makes Juneberry pies like this. And her cinnamon rolls are top notch."

By his rambling, Janie guessed his face was aflame too. She couldn't be certain though, as she wasn't about to look at him. She did, however, glance at John Brighton. Amusement danced in his eyes and tipped up the corners of his mouth.

Ahem. Time for her to exit.

Janie stood, brushing her damp palms down the front of her jeans. "Like I said. I have work to do." She turned for the sanctuary of her kitchen. "Just leave your plates when you're done."

"How much do we owe you?" Hunter called after her.

She waved her hand above her head as she pushed through the swinging door. "On the house."

Not because she couldn't use the money or because she actually felt like giving Hunter Wallace and his friend free pie. But because she couldn't face them again without a long, cool shower and a few words to her heart about latching on to stupid ideas.

She and Hunter and the label *wife* all tangled together was the chief of stupid ideas. And she should know that good and well—they'd already almost tried it.

It had ended with her heart in shreds.

Only idiots tried the same dumb thing twice.

Twenty-Two

"Janie Truitt." Brighton opened a new conversation as he settled in the new folding chair Hunter had bought from Mama B's general store when he'd gone to town.

They'd finished their pie, and Hunter had left two twenties on the table, knowing full well that Janie wouldn't offer him free food if she hadn't been absolutely mortified by his slip of the tongue. Then Hunter had led Brighton up the rough road, around the ridge, and down toward the minor lake, where his camp was. They'd spent the rest of the afternoon walking the footprint Hunter had laid out, talking business plans and possibilities and things that needed to be considered before Hunter moved forward. Hunter had made notes on a yellow legal pad, taking everything Brighton had to say with serious consideration.

There was no one he respected more than John Brighton.

But now, as they settled beside the crackling campfire Hunter had built, each with an MRE rehydrated with just-off boiling water, he wasn't so sure this was a conversation he wanted to have. With anyone.

Hunter cleared his throat. That was it. A man signal that should be understood—*skip it. That's an off-limits topic.*

"There was something between you, wasn't there?" Brighton either didn't get it or ignored the wordless cue.

Hunter tried to mask the scowl he felt. He also tried to look his superior officer in the eye. His stare only reached the man's chin. "Ancient history."

"Doubt it."

"What?"

"How long have you been gone from Luna? Four, five years?"

Hunter shrugged. "Something like that." Seven, if he counted his first few years of college. But who was keeping books?

"That's not ancient history. There is history there though. I could feel the crackle of energy between you two. And actually, even before, when I went in for lunch, I wondered . . ."

"Why would you do that?"

"They way she jolted straight when I mentioned I was here to see you. Like the sound of your name pushed on shrapnel somewhere in the region of her heart."

Hunter shoved a spoonful of rehydrated beef stew into his mouth while he turned his focus onto the flames in the Solo Stove.

"She's the reason you've barely dated, isn't she?"

He'd noticed that? Hunter searched back through the conversations he'd had with Brighton over the past year. Had they talked about Hunter's dating life—or lack thereof?

"Is she the reason you rarely came home?" Brighton didn't let up.

Hunter sighed. Obviously Brighton wasn't going to let this go. "There were several reasons. But yes, Janie Truitt was one of them." He forced himself to meet the man's steady gaze. "We were engaged before I signed with the navy."

Brighton nodded.

"She didn't want that life. Didn't want to leave Luna."

"It ended badly?"

"Yes. Very. She felt like I had broken promises—and since her dad skipped town when she was seven, it flared some long-held resentment." Hunter paused, making eye contact. "For the record, I didn't break any promises. I wanted her to come with me." There he swallowed, feeling the writhing ache of the night she'd returned his ring as if it had only happened moments before. He cleared his throat. "We . . . we've barely spoken since, and the few times we have . . . let's just say they weren't friendly."

Explosive. Those few conversations were explosive. To the point that Hunter had relabeled her name as *vampire* in his contacts list on his phone.

Strange, one would think he'd have blocked her number and deleted her information rather than labeling her a life suck and keeping her.

Again, Brighton nodded. "I could see how that would be difficult."

Hunter lifted his ball cap and let the night mountain air cool the tingling heat on his scalp before he replaced it. "The thing is, I didn't mean to say what I said down there." He gestured toward town. "Even if it's true." This time he looked straight at Brighton and let honesty surface in full. "I can't imagine another woman taking her place. Even after all this time and all the hurt and anger between us."

It was the first time he'd admitted it out loud and to its full measure. Janie Truitt was it for him. That had been true when he'd proposed, and it was every bit as true now.

He just didn't know how to live with it.

Hazel kept just the right amount of tension on the line as she waited for another hit—one that wasn't just a grazing pass. If she could land this one, that would make three trout that day. Enough to last her for the week. Later that afternoon, once she'd cleaned her tack, put it away, and grabbed a bite to eat, she'd take the dogs to the Juneberry patch. Hopefully, the bears and birds had left enough for her to pick a full bucket—or even two—since Janie had messaged her that she could use some more at the café.

Free pie in exchange for a few berries was a good deal, and Hazel didn't want to miss it.

The rumble of a vehicle neared, and the dogs let off a chorus of greeting. With her fingers still on the line, Hazel turned and watched Hunter's truck bounce toward the cabin. When it rolled to a stop, her brother cut the engine, and then he exited, as did another man.

John Brighton.

Hazel recognized the man's solid build, his erect posture, and his confident stride. As well as the kind but not overzealous smile he wore.

It tugged at the corners of her mouth. Turning back to her fishing pole, she cranked the reel with practiced ease, secured the hook on the third eye, and placed the pole on the dock. Then she strode toward the approaching men, meeting them on the dirt path.

Moose lumbered beside Hunter, his doggie expression happy and calm. The steady, faithful old friend. Ice and Cream danced around both men, yipping excitedly. Scout trotted to Hazel's side and sat. Ready to be a greeter. Or a protecter. Whichever the situation called for.

John Brighton held his hand out for Scout to smell, and then toward Hazel.

She shook it. "Surprise. I didn't know you were up this way."

"Just for a quick visit. I wanted to see what Hunter has going on. It's pretty exciting, I must say." John grinned broadly. "I've been sending pictures to Victoria, and she can't wait to come up and see for herself."

Hazel worked to keep a grin frozen on her face, but she turned a questioning glance onto Hunter.

Hunter looked caught.

She furrowed her brow. What exactly was John so excited about? Visiting? That was nice, but his enthusiasm was over the top. And Victoria was going to come?

Nice as she was, Victoria Brighton didn't not give off backwoods vibes. Hazel could not picture her being content to stay in Hazel's rustic cabin, let alone the shack.

"Oh, don't worry." John must have read Hazel's concern. "Victoria will wait to come until after the lodge is built. Sounds like maybe sometime next spring, if all goes well?"

Lodge? What lodge?

"With Bennett's experience in real estate and travel accommodations and Hunter's well-laid plans, we're thrilled to be a part of—" John's voice cut off sharply.

Hazel glanced at him and saw him look cautiously at Hunter.

Hunter stared at the ground, rubbing the back of his neck. When he finally lifted his eyes, he pinned them straight on her with a mix of plea and demand.

Please don't freak out. I'll explain. Don't embarrass me.

Hazel felt her temper rise like a hot summer afternoon. With some effort, she put her thoughts toward Bennett and what he would think if she just out and threw a fit right there.

He wouldn't think much of that. Call her a child, was what he would do.

She checked her words, measured her response. "I'm sure your wife will love it here, whenever she comes."

John cleared his throat. "Yes. Well, I just wanted to say hi to you and see your cabin before I head back down to Luna and then make my way back south."

Hazel nodded. The trio stood in a stiff circle. The panting of the three dogs filled the tense silence as John stepped back and shoved his hands into his pockets.

"Janie might need more berries," Hunter said. "I think she sold out of pie yesterday."

Hazel turned her gaze onto him and let it linger sharply. "Yes. She told me." She may have put a little more emphasis on the word *told*. Certainly Hunter would have gotten the message loud and clear.

Dang brother. Hadn't she just been over to his camp? Sat there and opened herself up to him, talking about taking Bennett to Black Gulch? Skipped rocks and let the conversation rove over personal stuff, like love? And he couldn't find a moment to mention he wanted to build a *freaking lodge* on her land?

Ahem. Their land.

Small detail. Didn't matter at the moment.

Hunter was a spineless coward. And Bennett?

Oh, he was gonna hear about this.

Twenty-Three

"You lied to me!" Hazel spat the words out like they were bitter herbs. She had met Bennett at the door to her cabin after hearing his vehicle come up the now-beaten road and park out back. She'd had a full day to fume, and she was ready to blow.

And . . . and oh boy, Bennett was in for it.

The man had the gall to look at her with confusion.

Stepping onto the deck, she shoved a finger into his chest and pushed until he stepped back. Now they were both out in the lowering late-summer sun.

"Don't stand there and stare at me as if you didn't know." Her pointed finger jabbed him every other beat. "As if you were innocent about it all. At least Hunter came clean."

"I have no idea what you're talking about." Bennet snatched her hand and lowered it back into her space. "Why don't you use your grown-up words and tell me what this is about?"

"Don't use your condescending language with me."

"Fine." He stepped to the side and moved to go into the cabin. "Why don't you go to the dock until you cool off, and then maybe we can discuss whatever it is I've apparently done without this blowing up in both of our faces. I had a large iced tea on my way here, and the bathroom is a necessity now. If you'll excuse me . . ."

"Oh no." She grabbed his hand. Didn't one bit care about what sort of drink he'd had on the drive from Bozeman. Liars could wet their pants as far as she was concerned. "You're not getting out of this with a bathroom pass."

Bennett growled. "Hazel, I'm not your puppy. I'm not even your brother. I'm not going to stand here dumb whipped while you have a temper tantrum. You want to have an adult discussion, I'm here for it. Even a fight, if that's what this is going to be. But until you quit making me play guessing games about whatever it is that set your pants on fire, I'm gonna go use the big boy's room."

"My brother is the problem!" Hazel stamped her foot on the deck, her boot making a loud smack against the wood plank. "And you knew about it! You knew about his plan for a lodge—even told him it was a good one—and you didn't even bother to tell me about it!"

Shutting his eyes, Bennett pulled in a controlled breath and let it out slowly. Then he nodded and refocused on her. Shoving his hands into his pockets, he turned to face her straight on. "Yes. I knew. Yes. I told him it's a good plan—because it is." He slid forward a half step. "I didn't lie to you about it."

"You didn't tell me." Her throat swelled, and her voice cracked. Dang it. She was mad. Mad should not bring tears—that looked weak.

But . . . he should have told her. How could he not have? It hurt. Should she tell him that?

That seemed so . . . small and vulnerable. Like she was fragile. Hurt equaled delicate. Hazel didn't want to think of herself as that. She was tough. Always had been. Would stay that way, even with Bennett.

Hazel thrust up her chin and glared into his dark-blue eyes. "I had to find out from that Commander Brighton guy. How could you let that happen? Instead of hearing it from my boyfriend, who claims to love me, I had to hear it from an almost stranger."

One whom she didn't even know was traveling all the way from Nevada to Montana to see Hunter.

Man! Why couldn't anyone tell her anything?

Another long sigh escaped from Bennett, then he reached one hand to cover her arm. "I had hoped you would hear it from Hunter himself." He squeezed her arm and then shook his head. "I really don't want between you two. Mostly because I'd prefer you two to work things out. You need to. You need each other, whether you want to admit it or not. But partly because I'm always going to be the bad guy if that's where I land."

She pinned her lips tight and squinted at him with all her pent-up fury. But she couldn't think of an argument.

Yep. He was the bad guy here. And perhaps the needing Hunter part was true too.

"Look, I wasn't exaggerating about needing the restroom," Bennett said. "Let me go take care of that, and then we can talk about this. Like adults. Two adults who care about each other. Okay?"

Ugh. There was that condescension again. Hazel really despised it when Bennett acted like she was a child.

He turned and took himself into the cabin, leaving her alone with her mad thoughts.

You're acting like a child . . . Do you hear yourself?

Hazel let a closed-mouth scream press through her throat, and then she pounded her way across the small deck, down the three steps, and toward the corrals.

Bennett could sit with his own self-righteous ego for a while. She'd take a ride. Maybe be gone until well after sunset, leaving him alone in that dark cabin. Wondering if she'd left him for the night. He still wasn't a great fan the dark. And he hadn't reached expert level at building fires.

Having fumed her way into the tack room, she gripped the large headstall for Mr. Big and ripped it off the wall peg.

You really want to lose Bennett?

Hazel froze as the thought seemed to come from outside of herself.

He's the best thing you've got going, and you know it. What other man would put up with your temper fits and strange personality? You want to lose his love?

Her shoulders slumped, and the hand that held the headstall dropped to her thigh. With her free hand, she forked her hair, pressing her palm to her forehead. The idea of losing Bennett—of the warm light of his love being snuffed out—made her gut tie up so tight that she got queasy.

She blinked against the liquid heat in her eyes. This wasn't exactly his fault. He didn't actually lie.

Why didn't he tell her though?

It felt like a betrayal. Not only because he'd kept it from her but because he approved of Hunter's plan when he certainly would have known she would not like it at all.

This is Hunter's land too, Zel.

But Hunter should have discussed this with her before going and finding investors and drawing up plans.

Exactly. That was exactly what Bennett had hoped for—and he didn't want to be in the middle of it. Was it fair of her to expect him to be the go-between?

She rubbed her throbbing brow. The anger that had fueled her temper cooled, leaving behind a scalding headache and a twisted-up heart. Replacing the headstall on the peg, she turned so that her back was to a corner in the room and slid down the wall until she sat in the dirt.

Why couldn't everything be easier? She hadn't wanted change, but she really liked the change Bennett brought into her world. She hadn't wanted Hunter to leave, but now that he was back, everything was one teetering move away from a complete explosion between them.

Why couldn't things just be the way she wanted them?

Child.

Hazel pressed her forehead into her fist while the name whispered through her heart.

Perhaps she'd never grown up. She was stuck as that scared, lonely teenager who couldn't make sense of life's blows. Or worse, she had grown up and she was simply a selfish, awful person.

She squeezed her eyes shut.

Outside, Bennett called her name.

She wasn't ready to face him like a grown woman yet, so she tucked herself back snuggly.

His footfalls neared and then stopped near the corral. "Hazel!"

Drawing a breath, she moved to stand.

The light streaming in the open door narrowed. Then it snuffed out completely.

Hazel froze, her heart stalled.

The sliding latch outside clunked into place. And then the sound of footsteps retreated.

Locked in.

She was locked in.

Bennett had locked her in!

Suddenly her heart was a running stallion, galloping, snorting, screaming into a storm. She ran the five steps it took to reach the door and began pounding.

"Bennett you . . . son of an ostrich!" Had she just used his ridiculous swearing substitute? "Let me out, dang it! Let me out of here now!"

She kept pounding and started kicking, yelling words Bennett would edit with animals.

Suddenly the door swung open. Hazel spilled out into the sunlight like a glass knocked off the table. Before her body planted into the dirt, strong hands caught her and set her upright.

Her fists kept right on pounding. Those naughty words continued spewing from her lips. And then she wiggled from his grasp and ran.

She was knee deep in the cold mountain waters of the lake before she stopped. Within three heaving breaths, Bennett splashed in behind her.

"Hazel." One hand curled around her elbow, and he tugged her. Once she was square with him, he cupped the other elbow as well.

She willed the burning liquid in her eyes to retreat. It refused, instead streaming down her cheeks. "I told you to *never* do that."

"It was a mistake. I promise." He shook his head, expression filled with concern. "I didn't know you were in there. You didn't answer me."

Her lips trembled. Not just her lips. Her body shook. She stepped back, but he wouldn't let her go.

"Why does this freak you out like this?"

"You locked me in!"

"I didn't mean to. You know I wouldn't do that. I would *never* intentionally be cruel to you that way, Zel." He stepped closer, pulling her arms into his chest. "Don't you know that?"

She swallowed.

The tears flowed like a stream during the spring melt, and she shook.

Bennett tucked her in close to his heart and held her fast.

With her eyes closed, her body held firm to his, the memory of that night set loose. And so did her mouth. The words tumbled out as if finally they were free and there was no stopping them.

"Hunter locked me in one night. He just . . . he just locked me in, and it was dark and cold and scary, and he wouldn't let me out. He told me to stay there and to be quiet or he would row me out to the middle of the almost frozen lake and dump me in." She sobbed.

And Bennett was silent.

When the memory played to the end and her words cut off, he held her close. "He left you there all night?" Something deadly cold iced his tone.

Hazel nodded.

Though he wrapped her securely with a gentle hold, she felt him stiffen. Like iron.

Later, after they'd gone into the cabin and changed, and Bennett had made sure she had some hot tea and warm blankets, he went to the door.

"Where are you going?"

"I'll be back in a bit."

"Bennett?"

The door clicked shut.

But Hazel knew exactly where he was going.

She should have never doubted it. Bennett was *for* her. Always. Even when it came to his buddy Hunter.

Twenty-Four

Bennett stormed his way across the ridge, not seeing the beauty of the late-summer afternoon trees nor hearing the consistent sound of the waterfall tumbling in the distance.

He only saw the trauma in his beloved's eyes as she'd sobbed. He only heard the roar of anger thundering in his mind. He only knew one thing: Hunter was going to pay.

Propelled by that drumbeat pounding through his head, his pace turned into a run. As his heart rate spiked, he felt the charge to get to Hunter's camp. Not the burn in his lungs nor the fire in his veins.

When he reached the old white-and-green trailer, he went straight to the door and pounded.

"What?" Hunter's annoyed call came easily through the tin can he called home. Then the door popped open.

Without a word, Bennett grabbed him by the shirtfront and jerked him outside. Hunter stumbled down the step and crashed into Bennett. Bennett jammed his shoulder into Hunter's chest to push him upright, and then using both fists, which were curled into the fabric of Hunter's sweatshirt, he shoved him against the side of the trailer.

"You locked her in the tack room!" he shouted, then pulled Hunter forward only to slam him back again. "You locked a thirteen-year-old girl in a cold, dark tack room for an entire night! What kind of worthless, sick human does that to his little sister?" Bennett banged Hunter up against the metal siding again, not feeling one bit bad when the other man's head smacked against the metal siding.

Hunter's expression went wide with shock, and then his brows pulled down. Understanding glimmered, then anger flared into his brown eyes. With palms pressed together, he pushed up in between Bennett's arms, reaching upward as if going into a dive, effectively breaking Bennett's grasp on him. With one strong and practiced move, Hunter had Bennett spun around so his back was against the trailer and one muscled forearm was pressed hard against his neck.

"I was protecting her!" Hunter growled.

"By locking her in a pitch-black shed for an entire cold mountain night?" Bennett seethed through the airway that Hunter was pressing against.

At his stifled words, Hunter eased back and let Bennett go.

"That's called abuse, you sick man, not protection." Bennett took a hard step forward straight into Hunter's space again. Likely, Hunter could take him down. He had military training, and he had a backwoods childhood to Bennett's city upbringing and office life. Didn't matter. Bennett would defend the love of his life, even if he came away broken and bleeding. "She's still traumatized. Freaks out if she even thinks the tack room door is going to shut on her. What the—"

"Better that than to have the memory of our drunk grandfather beating her."

Bennett froze. With a hard examination, he searched Hunter's face for a lie, an exaggeration . . . anything.

Anything that would indicate Hunter's implication wasn't . . .

No. There wasn't exaggeration there. Rather, there was pain the depths of which Bennett hadn't observed in Hunter before, and at the bottom of that agonized look was the truth. Gut-twisting nausea rolled hard.

"He . . ." Bennett's throat convulsed. "Your grandfather beat you?"

Hunter looked away. Then he turned, giving Bennett his back. With one hand, he lifted his sweatshirt and the T-shirt he wore beneath it until the skin just below his shoulder blade was revealed. There was a jagged six-inch scar, the skin puckered at the edges.

Bennett stepped back, the rage now redirecting itself toward a man he'd never met while horrified compassion took its place toward Hunter.

Fabric fell back over the healed damage, and Hunter readjusted his clothes, then he turned back to face Bennett.

"What happened?"

Hunter ran a hand down his face and then stepped toward the lake shore. "Pops started drinking after my mom and dad died. Usually, he'd stay out somewhere in the woods until he sobered up. He could be gone for days. Nan would say he was working the trapline—but I was old enough to know better. But that night—the one Hazel remembers—" Hunter's throat bobbed with a spasm, and he winced.

"That night he came home drunk?" Bennett filled in.

Hunter nodded. "Drunk and violent. Hazel had been off on a trail somewhere, and I knew there was going to be trouble—I'd seen it before—so when I saw her come back on Mr. Big, I helped her untack, and then I locked her in the tack room." He hung his head and rubbed his neck. When he looked back, tears leaked from his eyes. "I was sixteen, Bennett. Sixteen years old, and my grandfather was a big mountain man. I didn't think I could protect them both."

"Both . . . Hazel and your grandmother?"

Another nodded. "I did the only thing I could think of, because I knew Hazel was too stubborn to stay out of it. If she was stuck in the tack room, she couldn't get in the middle. She wouldn't see him like that, and she wouldn't get hurt."

Bennett shut his eyes, and behind his lids, he saw that jagged line of pinched flesh on Hunter's back again. This changed things—didn't make Hazel's trauma any less valid or difficult, but it changed what he thought about Hunter. When he opened his eyes, he found Hunter rubbing the streaks of wetness from the sides of his face.

"I know she thinks I was mean. I know she still thinks I'm selfish. But I'd rather she think that than remember what happened that night." He swallowed, and his throat visibly convulsed. "She and Pops had been close. He used to call her his little mountain girl, and she'd go work traplines with him when he was doing okay. I didn't want her to—" His voice cut hard.

He didn't want Hazel to know the man as a violent drunk. Remember him that way. Bennett nodded. "What happened? That night, I mean."

"He went after Nan—she ended up with a split lip and a bruised back. You can ask Hazel about that—she'll remember. Nan told her she was up on a chair cleaning the top of the cabinets and lost her balance."

"What about you?"

"I got between them, and Pops unleashed his drunken furry. I fought back, and a glass was broken. At some point we ended up on the floor, and I rolled on top of it."

Another hot round of queasiness rolled through Bennett's gut. "Did you get stitches?"

Hunter nodded. "After Pops knocked himself out on the counter, we dragged him to the bedroom and then Nan stitched me up."

"It's a miracle it didn't get infected."

"They'd lived off grid since forever—they were pretty self-sufficient. Nan cleaned it, and the next morning, after Pops came to and took off, she sent me down to town for a doctor to make sure everything was done correctly."

"That's when you let Hazel out?"

Hunter nodded. "First crack of dawn, I swear." Pleading and regret seeped from his expression.

"She didn't notice that you were hurt?"

"She was too mad." Hunter shook his head and rubbed his neck. "Said she hated me and never wanted to see me again. I stayed away until the bruises were mostly healed. She never knew."

Bennett rubbed his forehead. Man.

Man!

Those Wallace kids had lived a tough life. He ached for them both—for the awful memories they had and the struggles between them they still wrestled with. For several heartbeats, Bennett shut his eyes . . . *God, do You see them? This mess, these deep wounds . . . they need You.* Hot moisture rimmed his closed eyes as he prayed.

After a long exhale and a new grip on his emotions, Bennett looked back at Hunter. "You didn't tell anyone in town what really happened?"

"No." Hunter's quiet response was loaded heartache. "I told Mama B that I'd fallen from the roof—something she'd believe because we were forever patching holes up there. She kept me in town with her for about a week, and that was that."

"What about Janie? Did she know?"

Hunter pressed his lips tight and stared out at the light shimmering across the water.

Janie knew, then.

The knowledge cut sharp as Bennett considered what it meant for a man to have a woman know his deepest scars. His worst memories. The things that could break him and reduce him to tears. And then to lose her, to have her treat him with contempt . . .

Bennett rubbed his chest.

"Pops took off and never came back," Hunter said quietly. "It took two weeks before anyone started looking for him. They found his body at the bottom of Black Gulch. It was ruled a . . . a suicide."

God! Bennett winced while he silently shouted to heaven.

Why was there such awful brokenness in this world? How could people be so cruel to each other? He knew from his own troubled past that no one escaped the ugly parts of life. But to see it afresh now, in the woman he loved, and now in her brother? It made the ugly truth so much more real. And more difficult to reconcile.

How could one search for the goodness of God in a world cloaked in darkness?

In that moment, Bennett didn't have answers. No words that could comfort or ease or do anything. There was only this silent ache and a plea toward heaven for . . .

Something.

Healing.

Redemption.

Yes. Both of those things, for all of their shattered hearts.

Hunter sniffed. Bennett reached across the gap between them, once against gripping the thick material of his sweatshirt, and pulled his friend into a hug. The kind that he'd longed for from his dad since the day his dad had left. Strong and fierce. The kind that said *You're not alone. I'll fight with you.*

In that moment a bond of brotherhood sealed tight. Bennett would fight for Hunter, just as he would fight for Hazel. And he would start on his knees. Because one thing had been made clear over the past year—only true light consumes the darkness.

He'd grown tired of being afraid of the dark. He was tired of it for all of them.

Hunter pulled back, wiped another patch of wetness from his face, and sniffed again. "You can't tell Hazel that last part. About Pops. She doesn't know that he—" He swallowed hard.

That he took his own life.

Shaking his head, Hunter drew in a breath and then finished. "She doesn't need to know how he died, and she doesn't need to know where they found him. We told her he died on the line, where he was the happiest." He pinned a firm stare on Bennett. "We spread his ashes where we had done so for our parents. That's all she ever needs to know."

Bennett looked at his feet.

"I mean it, Bennett." Hunter squared to him. "I know you love her. Don't burden her with our Pops's sins."

Slowly Bennett nodded. Then he looked back at Hunter. "She needs to understand why you did what you did."

Hunter looked back over his shoulder. Back to the waters of the lake.

"It's time, Hunt. She's a grown woman, and she can handle that much."

After a stalled silence and a long-drawn breath, Hunter nodded. "Do what you think is right, Bennett."

"I think she needs to know how much you love her." Bennett covered Hunter's shoulder and squeezed. "It will matter to her, Hunt. I promise you, it will."

It could be the starting point. The dawning of the redemption Bennett longed for the Wallace siblings to find.

Lord God, let it be so.

Twenty-Five

Hunter collapsed into the sling chair. The old canvass fabric groaned in protest—and in warning. A time or two more of Hunter's full weight might just be a time or two more too many. He should go get the new chair he'd just bought out of the storage compartment.

But he wasn't thinking about that now. And his emotions had wrung him to the point of exhaustion.

Rubbing the thick mess of his hair, he absently noted that this was the longest he'd had it in years. Might be time for a haircut.

Might be time for a great many things.

An honest conversation with Hazel. And an apology for the stunt he'd pulled last fall.

A heart-to-heart with Janie. If she'd allow it—which wasn't likely.

But in that moment, the pressing call on Hunter's soul was for the letters. How could ink and paper seep so profoundly into a man's mind? How could mere words stir his soul, making him ache with longing and reach for a hope so dangerous it made him tremble? Hunter couldn't say, but it didn't matter. Finding the last bit of energy he had, he stood, strode back to the trailer, and fetched the handful of pages from a drawer beside his cot. Then, standing just outside of his trailer, he started at the beginning.

Hunter,

I can't say that I've done this before, but I feel the call of God to do so.

First, let me speak from the depths most men refuse to reach into. You have become as a son to me, and I care deeply what happens to you. I grieve that I will no longer be your commanding officer as much as I grieve that you will no longer be a part of the navy. It seems unfair, and truthfully, I have questioned God's wisdom in allowing this.

That might seem bad—for me to question God. I have the sort of relationship with Him, however, to know that He is patient with my feeble understanding. I also have the sort of relationship with Him to know for certain that He has not lost control over your life or mine. What He allows, He can use for good. Perhaps we simply need to surrender.

With that in mind, and with the conversation we have just had about you returning to Montana, I feel the nudge to surrender you. I hate to see you go. I'd rather you spend every Sunday afternoon at our table, and after the meal we continue our journey through the Proverbs. But I am not God, and I don't always know best. And as I've admitted that to the Lord, He has given me a word through his Spirit.

That word is for you, and it is this:

Return.

So though I don't want to, I am saying it to you: Return, Hunter. Go back to the lake, to your sister, and to the past you wanted so desperately to leave behind. There is something there, and since I know that God is good and He does good, I must believe that whatever it is He has for your return is good.

As you go, know you will be held fast in my prayers. And by our love. And remember, I love you as a son. Whatever you need, anytime, anyplace, I am only a phone call away.

John

Though it had been months since Hunter had first opened that letter, and many readings since, Brighton's words still plunged the full depth of Hunter's heart and dredged up emotions that seeped from his eyes. For a boy who didn't have a father, being called *son* by a good man was everything. For a boy who spent his adult life running, being told to return home was terrifying. And for a boy who didn't believe love could be selfless or enduring, having it freely poured without qualification was a marvel.

In all the months that Hunter had met with John, had listened to him talk about God, and had searched with him the life wisdom from Proverbs, nothing had been more compelling than that letter. It had not left his mind since the first reading. Now, all bars fell, any denial silenced.

Hunter wanted to know John Brighton's God.

Lowering the top letter, Hunter bent his knees until he was sitting on the step in front of his trailer door. He exhaled, allowing all the ugliness and gloom that had gripped him with Bennett's explosive visit to drain. As he leaned his head against the cool metal of the trailer, he shut his eyes and recalled the conversation between him and John while they drove back down to Luna for his departure.

"The lodge is a good plan, Hunt. I'm glad you feel like you can start a new life here." John paused, holding a meaningful look on him. *"But to be honest, I'm not certain that is the reason you were sent back. At least, not the whole of it."*

Hunter had swallowed. Then he nodded.

"Things aren't well with you and your sister, are they?"

"No, sir."

"She didn't know about the lodge before I spilled the beans, did she?" Heat burned against his face "No, sir."

"I'm sorry about that—I had no intention of making things worse."

"I know."

"And what about Janie?"

"We . . . Janie and I . . . like I told you last night . . ."

"Yes. You were engaged."

"It ended a long time ago. Badly."

"Hmm." John took a swig of his coffee. "From what I saw, things are still not good—but I would not call them over."

Hunter jerked a look onto John. He'd told him that he wasn't over her. What was his angle in bringing it up again?

Brighton chuckled. "Not by a long shot. Not for you and not for her."

"You don't think she's . . ."

"No." He held eye contact. "Blushes every time you speak, can't look you in the eye. Runs away at the earliest convenience. She might be ripe mad at you, but she's not over you."

Hunter could hear the roaring of something like spring thunder in his ears while his heart throbbed.

The mere possibility . . .

They pulled onto the dirt main street in front of the Pantry, and stepped out of Hunter's truck.

John gave him a firm handshake and placed a hand on Hunter's shoulder. "You were sent back for some reconciliation. Don't put if off."

Hunter nodded, and then dared to meet his eyes. "Brighton?"

"Yes?"

"There's something else I need you to tell me."

"What's that, son?"

The term *son* enveloped Hunter with exactly the security he needed to ask . . . "Your God . . . how . . . I want to know . . . I want . . ."

"You just believe, Hunter. Believe on the Lord Jesus Christ—tell Him that you do, and that you want Him to be the Lord and God of your life—and be saved."

Hunter opened his eyes and put his attention back on the letters in his hand. He shuffled to the fifth one down. It was in there—John had written something similar to what he'd spoken two nights past.

We are told in Acts how we can know Christ, son. There is quiet a scene written in Act 16:31—I hope that you'll dig out that Bible that I gave you and read it. In that story, you'll find this verse: "Believe on the Lord Jesus Christ and you'll be saved." Saved from the punishment for your sins—and eternity apart from God in hell. Forgiven for all the wrong. Redeemed and brought into a new life. Hunter! A new life!

"If anyone is in Christ, he is a new creation. The old is gone; the new is come." That's in the Bible too—2 Corinthians 5.

Read it, Hunter. And believe it.

I have no greater prayer for you than that.

Hunter looked up as the light of the rising sun warmed his face. He felt it. The newness.

Because he believed. And John had been right—it was like dawn had broken over the dark horizon of his soul.

Twenty-Six

Bennett took his time wandering back toward the cabin. Hunter's side of the story changed things. Now instead of livid, he just felt heartbroken. For both Hunter and Hazel. For the wreckage of their childhood, the loss of their parents, and the ensuing brokenness their grandparents had suffered.

The yearning to fix things somehow grew powerfully. What could he do though? He couldn't be the go-between for the Wallace siblings all the time—the recent fight between himself and Hazel was proof. But on this, maybe he could be the bridge.

The need within his heart was for more than that. He wanted to *be* there. Right beside Hazel in all things, every day. Able to take her in his arms when she finally collapsed into the need for shelter. Ready to be her refuge.

Because Bennett had resolved to live a God-centered life, though that could only happen if . . .

Maybe she was ready. Maybe, though it had started in fury, these storms had been a breakthrough for them. Had she not taken him to the one spot on this land that she'd not dared go to before? Had she not trusted him with the things that had haunted her and fractured her heart? Had she not sobbed against him?

Those were no small steps.

His mind whirled as he drew nearer her home.

Could be their home. The place where they could be one flesh, sharing this life until death. Secure in the promise, living the commitment.

A tremor rippled through his chest. Beyond words, that was what he wanted . . .

Movement stirred from the right, where the dock met the calm waters. Scout popped her head up and then barked. Ice and Cream saw him break from the tree line and came running. From his spot on the deck of the cabin, Moose lifted his head and let one greeting bark loose into the clean mountain air.

All was welcoming, like home.

Time changed so much. Rather than fearful panic, Bennett met the dogs who bounded at his legs with pets and "good dogs!" He smiled at Moose, calling "Hey, buddy!" When he glanced back at Scout, he felt keen approval as the pup remained faithful beside Hazel.

It felt right. Like family. A life he wanted with all his heart.

A sense of rightness and confidence billowed as Bennett strode toward the dock where Hazel stood, arms wrapped around herself, waiting for him. The late-morning sun backlit her honey hair, making it glimmer golden while it danced on the piney mountain breeze. The image chiseled in his mind—this mountain woman who was tender-tough owned his whole mind, body, and heart—and he could not imagine a more beautiful sight. If he were a more impulsive man, he would come before her in that moment, down on one knee and plead for her to make his heart's longing a reality.

But there was the matter that had sent him storming through the forest earlier that morning. She would want to know what was said and done between him and Hunter, and she needed to know the full story that Hunter had shielded her from. At least, most of it.

Euphoria plummeted. It was bound to be an emotional conversation—if Hazel would allow herself to feel. And man, did Bennett hope she would. She needed to. Hazel needed to drain the sludge of everything she'd kept bottled up tight about that night, and she needed to allow herself to feel Hunter's side. Her brother's desperation to keep Hazel out of the chaos, even if that meant locking her away. His ache at having carried both the memory of their drunken grandfather's fury and the ongoing resentment Hazel had held toward him for a situation she didn't fully understand.

Please, let her hear...

Bennett swallowed as he stepped onto the dock. When he was in reaching distance, he gripped both of her shoulders and pulled her into his chest. Her small hands curled into his button-down shirt as she rested her head against him.

"What happened?" she asked.

Wrapping her into a full embrace, Bennett inhaled the smell of sunshine and forest from her hair and then kissed the top of her head. "Hunter told me the whole story."

Her whole body went ridged. "Was he sorry?" she spat.

Bennett sighed. "Zel, honey, I need you to listen, okay?"

She pulled away and pinned a sharp look on his face. "What does that mean?"

"It means that yes, Hunter is sorry. He's devastated, if you want to know the truth, but not only because he feels bad about you being locked in the tack room that night. There is so much—" The recall of Hunter's tears pushed a surge of emotion into Bennett's throat.

He cleared it and started again. "There's more to what happened than you realize."

Skepticism clouded her expression.

"Do you remember him leaving for a while after he let you out the next day?"

"Yes. Ran off like a guilty rat."

Bennett shook his head. "Do you remember your grandmother having bruises?"

Hazel's brow pinched as she stretched toward recall. "I . . . I remember a few times, maybe?"

"That week, she had a bruised face—a split lip. She told you she slipped from a chair when she was cleaning something high. Sound right?"

Biting her lip, Hazel shrugged. "What does that—"

"She lied to you." Bennett regripped her shoulders. "Your grandmother didn't slip, and Hunter left for a week because he had a deep cut on his back that needed medical attention."

"What? Why?"

"Your grandfather came back from the trapline drunk and violent. That was why Hunter locked you away. He was trying to keep you safe. And when your grandfather hit your grandmother, Hunter intervened. He ended up being cut by broken glass."

Hazel shook her head in denial. Slowly at first, and then more vehemently. "My grandfather would not have done that."

"Zel." Bennett stepped nearer, pressing his forehead to hers. "Hazel. Please listen. Please don't shut out the truth because it's ugly. Your brother did the best he could to shield you from it. He didn't want you to know about your grandfather's drinking, and he didn't want you to get caught in the middle of something violent that night."

The woman beneath him trembled, and a rogue tear escaped, trickling down the side of her nose and landing on her tightly pressed lips. Something in her silence said that she knew the truth of what had been said. Like things were sliding into place, and though she didn't want them to, they fit.

"He loves you, Zel." Bennett held her face with his palms and tenderly brushed the ridge of her cheekbones. "Hunter only wanted to take care of you."

She sniffed, then straightened to step out of his hold. "Why didn't he ever just tell me?" Swiping at another rolling tear, she stared toward the opposite side of the lake, in the direction Hunter had claimed for his camp. "If that was all true, then he should have said."

Bennett sighed. "Go talk to him. Ask him yourself. Ask to see the scar on his back—it's jagged and ugly. And if you don't believe him after that, go talk to Janie—"

"Janie?" Hazel whirled around, the name a blade off her tongue. "Janie knows?"

"She knows why Hunter spent a week down in Luna after that night."

"Why would she never say anything to me?"

"My guess? Because she was honoring the wishes of the boy she loved."

Hazel's mouth closed, and the granite of her expression softened.

Bennett dared to close the gap between them again, this time taking her hand. "Maybe it's time to deal with the past and then let it go."

Biting her lip again, Hazel's attention drifted back toward the opposite shoreline. Slowly she nodded.

"There's healing, you know?"

She said nothing.

Bennett continued anyway. "And then there's life." With gentle fingertips, he brought her chin around so she would look at him. "I want us to have a life, Zel," he whispered.

Her eye grew round, expression melting into something soft and lovely.

Could that mean . . . was she . . .

The possibility was too wonderful to pass by. Bennett cradled her face, brushed her mouth with the softest kiss, and pulled away enough to capture her gaze again. "I want to marry you, Hazel."

She stared at him, the tenderness in her eyes cooling into something wild. Something frightened. "Bennett . . ." His name was a rebuke. A rejection.

An arrow that pierced his heart clean through.

Bennett pulled in a sharp breath. "That can't surprise you."

She folded her arms across her chest. "I . . . I'm not the kind of girl who marries." She shot him an accusatory glance. "You know that."

"I don't know any such thing. You're the girl *I* want to marry."

Turning toward the lake, she gave him her back. Bennett pushed forked fingers through his hair and gripped. He shouldn't have asked. Not yet. It was just that she'd seemed . . .

"How can I trust that it's me you want and not all of this?" Hazel spread her arms wide, indicating the land of her inheritance. Of her love.

The impact of her subtle accusation hit like a sledgehammer, and sparks of fury flew wild. Bennett pulled back, the blood flowing through his veins fire. He offered his love, his heart, told her she was the girl he wanted forever, and she came back at him with insult?

His fists curled at his side. "Oh yes. That is what this has been this whole time. The whole reason I've uprooted my comfortable life in Chicago, left a successful business I built myself, and started over in the wilds of Montana. All so I could get your freaking land!"

He paused, and she turned to face him. Bennett pinned a hard glare on her. "If that's all I had wanted, I could have just sued you last fall and been done with it."

Hazel shrank as he set free his anger, but he didn't stop.

"Nothing is more important to you than this lake. This land. Is it? Not me. Not your brother. Not anyone. It's only this land. You love it, and only it." He shook his head. "It is your obsession. One day you might figure out that this piece of ground and water is all you have. You'll have spent your whole life alone, clutching it with everything you have, and you'll wonder why it feels so empty. And that will be your fault." Bennett trembled as he finished.

And hated that he'd said any of it.

Hazel's shoulders curled inward and shook.

Man. Oh man, it hurt. The pain seared inside his chest . . . the pounding of his heart was every beat an ache. Bennett exhaled the last bit of his temper, and full remorse settled in like a gaping hole.

"Hazel." He took a half step toward her. "I'm sorry."

"I didn't mean it." She choked the words as she gave him her back.

Bennett suspected that, actually, she did mean it. She was scared he'd take away the one thing she had, this land. She didn't understand he meant forever, no backing out. Once again, he gripped the hair at the top of his head.

This had been such a mistake.

"I can't think about anything right now." Hazel turned to face him again, her expression now pleading, her wispy voice wounded and scared. "Everything is changing so fast. Please. Let me process what you've told me about Hunter. About Pops. Let me take in the idea of Hunter's lodge and what that will mean."

Lowering his hand, Bennett nodded. Hazel slid back to him, her fingers a caress as she ran them up his arm. "Please, let's not change anything between us." Those eyes, currently mossy green, did more than her touch to reach into his heart and squeeze.

This woman. She did own his love. Even when she was breaking his heart.

Bennett nodded. "For now," he rasped.

Hazel winced, though she tried to cover it up by tucking herself back against his chest. Her arms curled tight around him, and he held on to her.

For how long?

A loaded question. Bennett did his utmost to brush it to the furthest corner of his mind.

She would come around. He just needed to keep loving her.

And he would. He swore it to God Himself. He would love Hazel Wallace until the day he died.

Even if it killed him.

TWENTY-SEVEN

Hazel absent-mindedly watched while the bushy tails of Ice and Cream swished through the late-summer seed heads of the grasses that were allowed to flourish in this open section of land. Ahead, the large stand of pines on her right, and one of aspens on her left, created a framed view of Elk Canyon Pond. She paused, breathing in the crisp morning air full of the distinct aroma of burning pine. And dusted with a hint of last night's rain. It was both fresh and musky, an odd combination that had never struck her so until that moment. This view had never struck her as anything other than a passing beauty until that moment either.

But she saw it with new eyes. With an intentional lens toward Hunter's hopes and plans.

Borrowing his vision, and Bennett's, she could see it. The natural grandeur—the part she'd never had trouble viewing—and the wonderful possibilities for Hunter's lodge.

Perhaps Hunter had a point. A valid vision for the future.

Yes, Hazel truly wanted to preserve what was naturally glorious. Her few trips to Chicago had served to steel that determination. The last thing she wanted was to mutilate the beauty that she lived among for the sake of progress and profit. But there was that other part—the selfish part. The one that simply wanted to keep what she felt was hers only for her.

But it wasn't all hers.

After these several weeks of wrestling—with other profound revelations mixed in—she was coming to understand that. That she was a selfish woman who, intentionally or not, disregarded the feelings and needs of others.

One day you might figure out that this piece of ground and water is all you have. You'll have spent your whole life alone, clutching it with everything you have, and you'll wonder why it feels so empty. And that will be your fault.

To her dying day, she would hear the reverberations of Bennett's bitter accusation. The one that followed the ugliness of hers toward him—that he was only after her land.

She didn't want to come to the final chapters of her life as a lonely woman who had lived out Bennett's angry prophecy. With her whole heart, she wanted to spend life loving Bennett and savoring the comfort of his love.

But marriage?

Her feet stopped cold on the trail as the idea sent another fissure of anxiety through her being. Her heart pounded recklessly even as she thought of the possibility.

She had witnessed Nan live out her wedding vows. As much as Hazel loved Pops and was Pops's little mountain girl, she could see it wasn't a great deal for Nan. Truth was, the tale Bennett had shared from Hunter's side of the story of that awful night when Hunter had locked her in the tack room really shouldn't have surprised her as much as it had. Though she had only been a young teen, she had figured out why Pops would disappear for days—sometimes weeks—on end. She'd found the empty bottles in Pops's secret hideaway near the old access road. It was one of the reasons she never trekked that direction, even if it would have made getting to and from Luna easier.

She didn't want that life. And there weren't guarantees. Case in point, Pops hadn't always been that way. Hazel was certain of it.

What if Bennett changed? What if life threw him under the bus and he broke the way Pops had? Where would that leave her?

Trapped.

Hazel plunged her stride forward again, this time at a less leisurely pace. One might think she was trying to get away from something . . .

The idea of it was simply terrifying. Infinitely more so than being trapped in a dark shed for a whole cold night.

Which left her and Bennett and their relationship a big, heart-twisting question mark. That day at the dock hadn't been the first time he'd mentioned marriage. Just the first time he'd said it outright—that he wanted to marry her. It hadn't been a proposal, but her response couldn't be taken for anything less than a refusal. Which left them . . .

Dangling. Twisting in the dead space of the undefined.

Maybe it left them broken. By the stiltedness of the phone conversations they'd shared in the past few weeks, Hazel would say that was more than a maybe. And she didn't know how to fix it.

She paused as Hunter's trailer came into view. There was so much in her life she didn't know what to do with. But there was Hunter. Right there in front of her. Returned and bound to stay.

It was time for some reconciliation.

A yip and then a bark sounded from the other side of the pines near Hunter's trailer. Ice and Cream had made her approach known to her brother. Scout glanced up at Hazel, looking for the *go on* signal from her, which she gave. The pup sprang ahead, darting to join the other dogs. Moose had stayed behind at the cabin, as he often did. That day, Hazel felt his absence keenly. The big boy was an old man, and he didn't move like he used to. And for the past two weeks, Moose had sulked around the cabin. Like he was grieving all over again.

How did dogs know?

Hazel had tried to reassure him. Patting his massive, hairy head, she'd say, "He'll be back, boy. He just had to go see his dad . . . Just wait. He'll come back."

She did not feel at all sure of that claim.

With a shuddered breath, Hazel moved toward Hunter's camp, shoving away the image of Moose lying on the small deck, his paws draped over the top step, chin resting on his legs. Eyes sad.

Willing Bennett to come back.

Please come back . . .

Three dogs barked in a chorus of excited calls, and then Hunter came around the back side of his trailer. "Hazel." His greeting was surprised, but in a good way, and he waved. "Look at you, making it to my side of the mountain."

The corners of her mouth tipped up. She came into his camp, noting that he kept it tidy, even if his home was a hunk of junk. Having waited for her to pass by, Hunter followed her toward the stone ring surrounding the tall silver cylinder of his Solo Stove.

"Have a seat." He motioned toward a new-looking yellow chair. Must have ordered it through Mama B. "Coffee is almost ready. Want some?"

Hazel shrugged. "Sure."

He busied himself with gathering another metal mug from the trailer and pouring the dark, steaming liquid. Once they both held a full mug, he sat back in his chair. "What brings your smile my way today?"

She would hardly say she was *smiling*. But he was cheerful, and she gave him credit for trying. With a careful gaze, she looked at the view—the smaller pond in front of them, the layers of hills beyond the opposite shoreline, the pine and aspen forest around them. "So this is the place, hmm?"

"For the lodge?" Hunter's tone held optimistic caution.

Hazel nodded.

His shoulders relaxed. "I think so. The road access is good. Fishing is excellent. There are several good trails. It's out of sight of your cabin and shouldn't interfere with your peaceful life at the big lake." Pausing, Hunter cast a hopeful glance her way.

She nodded again. "I can see it."

"Can you?" Pure shock carried those words.

For a moment, the world held still between them.

"Can you really, Zel?" Hunter whispered again.

Forcing herself to look at him, she nodded for the third time. "I . . . I have been selfish. This land is both of ours. And Bennett says that the lodge is a good idea—and he would know. That's his world."

"What about you?"

Shrugging, she blew out a breath, then stood and walked to the waterline. "I'll adjust."

"I'll make sure that you're not bothered. I promise, Zel. But—" Hunter came to stand at her side. "But we could be in this together. I wasn't after this for just myself, I swear. You're a good guide, and you know this land better than anyone."

She winced as she heard the mix of kindness and longing in his voice. He really was trying to look after her, to provide for her. And he wanted her in this with him.

That was . . . profound.

He had been *for* her all along. Even with that stupid stunt he'd pulled with Bennett.

Even with the night she'd spent locked in the tack room.

Looking up at him, she caught his eyes. "Why didn't you ever tell me the truth about that night?" She had to blink against the sudden surge of liquid warmth in her eyes.

Hunter's focus moved toward his feet. Shoving his hands into his pockets, he shrugged. "You always loved Pops—the two of you were close. I didn't want to tarnish his memory for you."

Tentatively, Hazel reached for his arm. The moment her fingers made contact, he stepped closer and wrapped her with it. She tucked herself close to him, and his hold grew in strength. After several long, healing moments, he kissed the top of her head.

"Haven't seen Bennett in a couple of weeks."

"He went back to Chicago to visit his family."

Hunter's silence hinted that he could detect her half-truth. "You two okay?"

A shudder rippled through her whole body. "I don't know."

"Oh, Zel." He turned to pull her into a full hug. And then he let her cry in the safe silence of his brotherly embrace. "No matter what, sis, you have me. You always have me."

She had no idea how long those tears ran. All she knew was that when she stepped out of the refuge of his arms, her whole face was wet, and things between them felt clean.

Like a new beginning.

"I've learned some things this year, Hazel."

She wiped her face with both hands. "Yeah?"

"Yeah. I want to tell you about them."

"Now?" A wall of resistance climbed, and Hazel felt herself stiffen.

Hunter studied her, then smiled gently. "No." He pulled her back and tucked her under one arm again. "Right now, let's just be."

After several moments, filled with the gentle lapping of water, the whisper of breeze in pines, and the occasional churl of a squirrel, Hazel leaned the side of her head in against his chest. "I'm glad you came back, Hunter."

He squeezed her shoulders. "We're going to be okay, Zel. You and I, we'll be all right."

Hazel believed him. She had no idea how things would work out with her and Bennett. And she was still terrified of this lodge business Hunter was going to bring up the mountain. But at the end of the day, she had this: she and Hunter were okay.

And that was a very, very big thing.

THE END

(For now ..)

I hope you enjoyed this return to Elk Lake. I've been told this story isn't what readers expected... and I get it! But I hope it found a place in your heart, even if it wasn't where you thought this book would end up. And rest assured, we have so much more to discover at Elk Lake Canyon! Hunter and Janie, Bennett and Hazel... their stories aren't done!

I have so much more to share with you. Keep watching for the release of those stories in the next few months. You can preorder book 3, Lake Shore Splendor now!

I hope you've enjoyed this second book in Redemption Shores. Would you please leave an honest review to let other readers know what you think? Thank you!

Teaser for Lake Shore Splendor

Arms crossed, Bennett leaned hard against the thick scrolled iron railing on the balcony overlooking the pool. The crystal-blue water, disrupted by Gemma and her friends playing in the water, however, w not in his line of view.

Bennett stared at his dad, eyes bulging, lips pressed hard.

Chip—*Dad!*—shook his head and chuckled. The sound was all condescension. "Don't gape at me like that, son."

"How should I gape at such a request?"

Dad leaned back against his thickly padded deck chair, an ankle crossed over one knee. His leather loafer bounced with the movement of his foot. "It's not forever. A semester, maybe. Perhaps the school year. Nathan needs a new scene before he gets involved with any more bad influences. And Gemma will adjust. She's easygoing that way." A smile that Bennett felt certain he'd used himself on several occasions smoothed over his dad's face. The one that sealed the deal more often than not. "Anyway, they're not trouble. Give them a pool or some kind of tech, and you basically never hear from them."

"Nice, Dad." Bennett straightened, pulling his weight off the railing, and glanced down at his younger half sister. Gemma favored their shared father—she had his ruddy coloring and a pair of adorable dimples that could likely gain her about anything she wished. She dolphin dove beneath the water, swimming after her dark-haired friend as they played a game of water tag. Her happy world was teetering, and the poor eleven-year-old girl didn't even know it.

Bennett shook his head. "There aren't a whole lot of private pools in Montana." He turned to pin a scowl on his dad, only to find the man had stood and now wore a pleading expression.

"Look, Benji."

"Bennett." Bennett held a stern expression on his dad.

"Son." Dad exhaled a long, dramatic sigh. "The truth is that Mindi and I probably are not going to make it. I've accepted it, but she wants this one last try. Figure after this long, I owe her that. This couple's retreat is . . ."

Bennett shook his head. A rising holy temper drummed in the depths of his soul. Honestly, he didn't care about his father's four-month-long intensive couple's whatever in Europe—except that was so Dad. Throw some money at a problem and hope it stuck.

If it didn't . . . eh. Oh well. Move on. Leave a wife . . . she'll get over it. Abandon some kids . . . they'd be fine with a padded bank account.

Who needed an actual dad?

How had this man claimed to follow Christ and had even pastored a church for seven years? The confounding mystery of that antagonized Bennett exceedingly. But at the moment the more pressing and exasperating puzzle was why his dad had thought Bennet would want to take on guardianship of his half siblings while Chip and his likely-soon-to-be-ex-wife took off for four months. Or longer.

And here Bennett had stupidly thought that when Dad had asked him to come and try again, he had actually meant what Bennett had meant—to be reconciled.

Bennett blew out a hard breath. "Dad, you *can't* do this to them."

Chip frowned. After a quick glance toward the pool, he shook his head. "They don't know about Mindi and me right now." He shrugged. "Who knows? Maybe they'll never have to know."

How could this man be so disgustingly cavalier about this? "They'll know something's wrong if you send them to live with me in Montana."

Another shrug. "Either way, they'll not be staying. The other option is a boarding school in New England."

"What?"

"Chicago isn't what it used to be, and Nathan, as I've already alluded to, has been finding trouble. He just needs different people around him . . . Anyway, the point is, either way they're going somewhere."

"Dad." Bennett huffed out the title with pure exasperation.

Chip stepped next to Bennett and covered his shoulder with one hand. Bennett had to discipline away the reaction to sidestep out of the man's touch. Resentment bubbled up from the deep storage of years' worth of anger. He flinched at the strength of the surging reaction.

And then he let his gaze rest on the copper-haired girl laughing in the water below. Hazel's face drifted through his mind. She would have been about the same age as Gemma when she lost her parents.

At least Hazel had had her brother to see her through.

Bennett swallowed. His chest ached. He had to clear emotion from his throat before he could speak. "I need to pray about this."

The hand on his shoulder squeezed. "Sure. Sleep on it, why don't you?" Then Chip clapped his back. "The guest house comfortable enough for you?"

With a glance over his shoulder, bypassing his dad's impassive face, Bennett looked through the glass French door that led into the guest suite above the pool house. It was nothing short of luxury. Something Bennett would have put in one of his more high-end resorts.

The tech industry certainly paid well. Much better than the church gig. Couldn't hurt that Mindi was an accountant in a highly prized firm used by the beyond-wealthy people of the Northern Shore.

"It's fine, Dad." It took work not to allow the sharp edge of his irritation to cut through his tone.

"Good." Dad turned, strode toward the padded deck chair, and stopped to snag his Eagle Rare Bourbon. Pausing, he raised his glass. "Can I get you one?"

"Nine is a little early for me." Bennett couldn't school the frown that pressed on his mouth. "Thanks."

"Suit yourself." He turned back toward the spiral stairs and descended as if he hadn't a care in the world.

"Dad!" Gemma's call broke through the splashing and giggles of the three girls in the pool. "Watch this!"

"Of course, princess." Dad's smooth reply rippled with adoration.

Bennett's stomach burned.

Gemma dove into the water and performed a handstand, her manicured toes pointing straight up to the clear blue late-August sky. Then she pulled them in as she executed a perfect flip-turn and sprang to the surface.

Chip clapped. "I give it a ten, baby doll."

Her smile stretched. "Thanks, Daddy."

"When you girls are done, I've ordered some of those yummy cinnamon crispies you like."

A round of squeals ensued from all three girls, loud enough to wake the perpetually sullen Nathan, who had not emerged from his bedroom before one in the afternoon any of the four days Bennett had been there. Likely because he stayed up until the wee hours of the morning playing on the new iPhone Dad had gifted him with as a back-to-school conciliatory prize.

How could Chip be this stupid?

He was buying them off. Just as he'd attempted to do with Bennett. And it was revolting.

Bennett wanted no part in aiding his dad's continued trek into the great abyss of self-indulgence. But those kids . . .

At least when Chip had abandoned Bennett, Bennett still had his faithful mother. Nathan and Gemma?

From what Bennett could see, Mandi wasn't much like his mom. Starting with the fact that she was willing to dump her teenage kids off on a stepson she barely knew. No, not starting there. Starting with the fact that over a dozen years before, with zero qualms, she'd been sleeping with a man who was married to someone else.

Nathan and Gemma would get washed out to sea in this churning storm of selfish living, and they would have no one to show them what real love and faithfulness looked like.

That possibility broke Bennett's heart.

KEEP READING! Order Lake Shore Splendor here.

Printed in Great Britain
by Amazon